CW00952568

Rough Waters and Other Stories
Facing Ethical Dilemmas

By
Richard Ned Lebow

Rough Waters and Other Stories: Facing Ethical Dilemmas

By Richard Ned Lebow

This book first published 2022

Ethics International Press Ltd, UK

British Library Cataloguing in Publication Data

A catalogue record for this book is available from the British Library

Print Book ISBN: 978-1-871891-37-9

eBook ISBN: 978-1-871891-90-4

Contents

DEDICATION

To Alex George (1920-2006) who first encouraged me to write fiction.

To Nora Franglen, Tony Grenville, Julia Pascal, and Amy Shuman for being so supportive of my efforts.

INTRODUCTION

What follows can be read as an introduction to my stories or a conclusion to them. It describes my incentives for writing, and puts the stories in personal, conceptual, and collective perspectives. I hope it provides a framework that enhances your reading experience. Some of you may want to form your own impressions and make your own connections across stories. I urge you to proceed directly to the stories and read my introduction as a conclusion.

All my tales address different ethical questions and dilemmas. They collectively make the case for a tragic approach to ethics. My characters must make or finesse ethical choices, some of them straight-forward, others involving very difficult trade-offs between seemingly irreconcilable but important goals. Alternatively, they require characters to commit to decisions or policies whose outcomes are uncertain. We are desperate to avoid dilemmas of this kind and prone to convince ourselves – often in the face of good evidence – that we can satisfy all of our desires or needs instead of making tough choices between or among them. We also tend to convince ourselves that our decisions or policies will succeed in proportion to the degree that we feel compelled to commit to them. A standard trope of Greek tragedy – think here of Oedipus – is that our decisions sometimes lead directly to the outcomes we are trying desperately to avoid.

The tragic view of life is rooted in an understanding that the world is to a significant degree opaque. We have at best a limited ability to control and manipulate it and our best efforts to do so often backfire. We are acted on at least as often as we are responsible agents, and efforts to enhance our agency and power can just as readily reduce them. Tragedy encourages us to confront our limits. It emphasizes human fallibility and vulnerability and the contradictions and ambiguities of agency. It shows us that we not infrequently initiate courses of action without being able to control them or calculate beforehand their consequences. It cautions against assuming that our own conceptions of justice are universally applicable and should be imposed on others. It warns of the dangers of over-confidence and perceived invincibility. It teaches us that wisdom and self-awareness can emerge from adversity and despair.

Tragedy offers a possible antidote to some of the most dangerous conceits of modernity. It can make people humble and cautious, and encourage decisions that pay as much attention to what can go wrong as to what we hope will go right. However, tragic understandings of politics or life will only appeal to people and leaders with courage to face that truth that we are to a large degree at the mercy of our physical and social environments. It is less a substitute for modern ways of addressing problems as a much-needed corrective. As with everything else in life there should be a balance, between self-interest and concern for others, risk taking and risk aversion, optimism and pessimism, overconfidence and lack of confidence, flying by the seat of the pants and acting on the basis of careful analysis and preparation, and focus on the benefits of action versus those of inaction. A tragic perspective also gives people a useful outside vantage point on their behavior and a focus on its longer-term consequences, even if they are ultimately unknowable. It compels us to recognize and accept uncertainty and responsibility in lieu of denying them.

My stories are intended to sensitize people to tragedy and its ethics. I set the scene with an exploration of the post-life of President Richard Nixon. The story asks if leaders should be held responsible to the same ethical code as ordinary people. Do their special responsibilities for the organizations and states they head give them leeway to act in ways that would be reprehensible if used to advance personal interests? My answer in a resounding no, which flies in the face of much conventional wisdom and most realist approaches to foreign policy.

"Nixon in Hell" has a very personal genesis. I remember few occasions in my life when I became seriously depressed. One of them was following the election of Richard Nixon in 1968. I had despised "Tricky Dick" for years and knew full well that he would escalate the war in Vietnam, not end it, and also do his best to slow down civil rights for African-Americans. In the spring of 1968 Henry Kissinger invited me to interview for a postdoctoral fellowship at Harvard. We met in in the Fifth Avenue apartment of Nelson Rockefeller, just across from the Metropolitan Museum of Art. "Rocky" had thrown his hat in the ring for the Republican presidential nomination and Kissinger was his chief foreign policy advisor. The reception room had glorious art on the walls but there was no opportunity to do anything but cast sideways glances at it. Kissinger asked me a few questions about my research and I told him how much I would enjoy a postdoc that would let me transform my dissertation into a book. Much to my surprise, he explained that the job in question was working for him, not for Harvard. He was likely to become national security advisor and was putting together a staff to take to Washington.

This was something of a bait and switch. I was also convinced that Rockefeller would lose the nomination to Nixon. Not to worry, Kissinger assured me, Rocky would pass him on to Nixon if this happened. The Republicans would almost certainly capture the White House and he would become national security advisor. I told Kissinger that I had read and been impressed by his article on Vietnam policy published a few months earlier in *Foreign Affairs*. In it he made an analogy to France and Algeria. De Gaulle came to power promising to keep Algeria French but once in the Palais de l'Élysée granted the former colony its independence and withdrew French troops. Kissinger suggested that the next President should follow this precedent as De Gaulle and France rose in stature in the aftermath. Kissinger leaned across the coffee table dividing us and said in his thick German accent: "Young man, do not believe everything that you read." He explained that he had written the article with Rockefeller in mind. Now that he would likely be working for Nixon such a policy would not pass muster. His boss would almost certainly escalate the war in the short-term.[1] "Do you feel comfortable with this course of action?" I asked. He smiled. I politely declined his job offer. We parted on friendly terms and when my first book appeared he wrote me a nice note.

My depression was warranted. Nixon and Kissinger prolonged the war, extended it to Cambodia, and then negotiated a truce that led to the very outcome they were trying to avoid. Many thousands of people died as a result. At home they violated the constitution and laws at will. Nixon won re-election but the Watergate scandal led to a series of revelations that compelled him to resign to avoid impeachment.

My depression only lasted a week or so after the election, although my concern remained acute until Nixon was driven from office. Along with millions of other Americans I experienced a great sense of Schadenfreude with each Watergate revelation, resignation, and conviction of former officials, although I was dismayed by Ford's pardon of Nixon and continuing suffering in Indochina.

As the saying goes, revenge is a dish best served cold. I did not write

"Nixon in Hell" until 2001, several decades after these events. I no longer remember the immediate catalyst for the story but do recall how good it felt, even after all these years, to condemn this violator of human rights and the constitution to the netherworld and imagine how he would react, what he would think, and how he would suffer. I did not have physical punishment in mind, but various offenses to his ego and fragile sense of self. To my surprise, Nixon coped better than I had expected. To the extent I tried to stay true to his character the story escaped my control. Nixon is a villain – there can be no doubt about that – but not an entirely unsympathetic one. There is another bad guy in the piece, but he will remain unnamed as I do not wish to give away the plot. He also gets his comeuppance, which was another source of satisfaction given his complicity in one of the greatest crimes of the twentieth century.

Nixon and his co-villain are representative of a class of people who violate norms and laws in the perceived interests of their institutions. The Catholic church went to great lengths to protect sexual predators among its priesthood, corporations regularly despoil the environment in the name of profits, and countries use violence allegedly in defense of the national interest – which, to be fair, is sometimes justified. Realists praise national leaders for acting this way, and some of the worst offenders – consider Henry Kissinger – are hailed as heroes rather than arrested and tried as war criminals. My story questions this double standard. It is one of two stories that were previously published*, in this instance at the outset of a book that argues that foreign policies at odds with conventional understandings of ethics are less likely to succeed.[2]

I believe similar arguments can and should be made about institutions and businesses. To some degree this ethical imperative is recognized in the form of hypocrisy. People who violate norms and laws do their best to justify their behavior in terms of them or with reference to some higher good. A good measure of the health of any society is the extent to which such people are scorned and treated as pariahs or criminals. Society is on the decline when their claims are accepted at face value by people too ignorant to know otherwise or willingly complicit because they expect to profit in some way by doing so – as many Republican officials did in publicly supporting Trump's false claim that the 2020 presidential election had

---

* "Nixon in Hell," was first published in *The Tragic Vision of Politics: Ethics, Interests, and Orders*, Richard Ned Lebow, (Cambridge: Cambridge University Press, 2003), ch. 2

been rigged. Society is weaker still when hypocrisy is no longer considered necessary because formerly unacceptable behavior has become increasingly acceptable.

"Surviving Tet," written in August 2021, continues my engagement with Vietnam. I wrote it in response to the American failure in Afghanistan and shambolic departure from Kabul. Images of these events mixed with those embedded in my memory of the costly and embarrassing evacuation of Saigon in 1975. I had first-hand experience of Vietnam during the War. I traveled around the country giving talks, interviewing people of all kinds, and seeing for myself what was happening on the ground. As you will see, it was not without risk.

Truth is said to be stranger than fiction. I am a firm believer in this cliché and offer "Surviving Tet" as evidence. Everything I relate is true but would lack credibility if presented as a short story. I have accordingly written up the first part as a narrative. I blend fact and fiction in the back half where I put words in the mouths of my interlocutors. They are real people, they have the affiliations I attribute to them, and they behaved just as I describe. All of this happened more than a half-century ago, so I have no recall of their actual words but do remember clearly the gist of what they said and the impressions they made. I have even more vivid impressions of my own and my wife's responses to Vietnam. Fascination and fear dominated. We were in a foreign country, one best described as semi-occupied, where the clash of cultures was evident in almost every social interaction.

We quickly understood that the dynamics of the conflict in Vietnam bore little relationship to their framing in Washington, D.C. The South Vietnamese army was utterly corrupt and all but worthless, as was government at every level. The U.S. was wasting money and lives, something apparent to many Americans in Vietnam, but back home generals and politicians alike were deluding themselves. So it was in Afghanistan. My narrative cum story highlights this difference and the varied responses of local American political and military officials to what they regarded as a no-win situation.

In *The Tragic Vision of Politics*, I argue that great powers are their own worst enemies and inflict far greater harm on themselves than do foreign actors.[3] Their power makes them arrogant and also less necessary – at least in the short-term – to adjust to unpleasant realities. It also stands in the way of learning from their failures. It is another manifestation of tragedy, provoked by hubris. For the ancient Greeks this was a category error; people believed they possessed the power of gods and could predict and control the future at will. Hubris was punished with nemesis, and this has been the recurring fate of great powers who overstep ethical boundaries in pursuit of hegemony.

The American national security elite learned little to nothing from the Indochina disaster and there is no reason to think they will do any better in the aftermath of Afghanistan. As I write, the media and many politicians are playing the blame game, as they did in Vietnam, and about the so-called "loss of China" before that. In part, this is politics, but it is also a kind of conspiracy across the party divide to avoid addressing these failures in a serious way. To do so would call into question America's self-image and the self-esteem of its citizens. No politicians will go down this road and intellectuals who try are largely ignored.

"Nixon in Hell" and 'Surviving Tet" also speak to my political agenda, as do most of my stories. I have been a professor for fifty-four years and for the first few decades most of my research focused on conflict management and prevention. I worked at City College of New York, Johns Hopkins, Cornell, the Naval and National War Colleges, and was scholar-in-residence in the Central Intelligence Agency during the Carter administration. In these positions I did my best to analyze and document the dangers of deterrence and of the American quest for hegemony. My research was ignored by the policy community because it was so different from and so contrary to the conventional wisdom. I got tired of banging my head against the wall and shifted my research agenda to the underlying political and psychological assumptions on which American national security policy was based. Both kinds of research resonated with and won plaudits from some segments of the scholarly community. I have now turned to fiction in the hope of reaching a wider audience.

"Foo Fighters" refers to the lights observed by pilots on American bombing missions over Germany late in World War II. Fighters would go after them only to have them turn at sharp angles and disappear at fantastic speeds. The army air force wondered if they were secret German weapons but could find no evidence for it once Germany was occupied. Only a few years later Americans began seeing flying saucers and tracking them on radars. One of the more popular postwar conspiracy theories concerns the alleged crash of an alien spaceship near Roswell, New Mexico, and the recovery by the air force of aliens or alien corpses. A close family member – former vice president of a leading software company -- swears that he was told by IBM engineers that they reverse engineered their 360 computer based on the computer in this alien ship. It seems inconceivable that a civilization capable of interstellar travel would be using a computer more primitive than those in your automobile and one, moreover, that relied on vacuum tubes! This tale illustrates how conspiracies play fast and loose, not only with fact, but with common sense. This does not stop them from spreading and people who hear them coming up with "evidence" in support.

Troubled by conspiracies, especially political ones, I wrote a novel – soon, I hope, to see the light of day. *Uninhibited Flying Objects* is a spoof on conspiracy theories. It slyly and humorously demonstrates the improbability of "deep state" conspiracies, their difficulty in execution, and the near-impossibility of being kept secret. "Foo Fighters" was originally its opening chapter. Readers convinced me to start with a later chapter so I pulled it from the book. I think it works well as a short story as it effectively questions key assumptions of conspiracy theories. The most outrageous one is that governments could coordinate vast efforts of some kind and keep them from the public eye. Governments, even authoritarian ones, are like sieves because officials at every level have all kinds of incentives to leak information. Tony, my hero, recognizes this truth and witnesses concerted and ultimately unsuccessful efforts by the air force – all historically true – to keep the unexplained phenomenon of Foo Fighters under wraps.

Conspiracies and hypocrisy are related. Those who indulge in hypocrisy and seek wealth or power by questionable means often support conspiracy theories to direct attention from themselves or to justify their behavior. The German right and Hitler famously propagated the *Dolchstoss* [stab in the back] lie that the German army was never defeated by the allies in 1918 but undermined by Jews and socialists. Present-day American Republicans continue this tradition. *New York Times* columnist Charles M. Blow observes that Republican politics have become oppositional politics.[4] They deny the science, attack the media, and spread conspiracy theories about scientists, the medical profession, and government. They wage war on facts as they stand in the way of their programs, especially their claims that tax cuts for the rich trickle down and benefit the poor. Donald Trump invented and spread the lie that Barrack Obama was born in Africa and really a Muslim.

Wikipedia offers a long list of other conspiracy theories promulgated by Trump and notes his support of diverse conspiracy theorists.[5] Trump's hangers-on and would-be successors follow his example.

"Foo Fighters" also questions the ethics of carpet bombings of cities and their wanton destruction of housing, public buildings, and non-combatant lives.[6] The Germans pioneered aerial attacks on civilian populations; Guernica and Rotterdam were among the first population centers to suffer this kind of destruction. German attacks on London were offered as justification of allied attacks on German cities and the allies paid the Germans back many-fold. Their raids reached their deadly peak in the two-day fire-bombing of Dresden in February of 1945, killing perhaps 25,000 people and creating between 100,000 and 200,000 refugees.[7] The fire-bombing of Tokyo and the atomic bombings of Hiroshima and Nagasaki were more destructive still. Tony, the hero of my story, is an uneducated fellow but no fool. He is not happy about killing civilians but has no choice. He has to do what is told, and comes to develop pride in his unit and solidarity with his crew and unit. He does his best to deal with this dissonance, in large part by trying to finish his tour of duty, return home, and put it all behind him. We are sympathetic with Tony, and he helps us understand how so many decent people in war-time do horrible things.

"Physician, Heal Thyself" is the first of my contemporary stories. Its theme is the ubiquity of passwords and the difficulty of remembering them, especially when they must be changed on a regular basis. My tale is disturbing for what it reveals about the social nature of illness and deviance. Most of us who are compelled to remember multiple, ever-changing passwords, struggle with this task and try to minimize the challenge by keeping crib sheets, using the same password at multiple sites, and passwords that are easy to remember. All of these moves are made at the expense of security, and can be self-defeating. My characters in the hospital ward have rebelled against the unreasonable demands that are being made on them. I am on their side. My university library demands not only a password, but code sent to a special device just to scan the catalog. Why shouldn't anybody be able to do this without a password?

Those in charge of security have strong incentives to require passwords for everything as it increases their responsibilities. So do the ubiquitous consultants who advise businesses and institutions on their security requirements. They have a strong financial interest in securitizing everything in sight. I am not suggesting that security is unimportant. Hackers have made many millions by bringing businesses to their knees. Their break-ins have also compromised the personal data of millions of people. Only some of these problems are attributable to bad passwords. Despite repeated warnings people still choose passwords that are easily guessed, like those that feature their names or dates of birth, or are readily conned into giving their passwords to others. Most serious break ins are due to security barriers that are inadequate, out-of-date, or easily penetrated by hackers. The imposition of passwords on sites where security is unnecessary, the proliferation of multi-step log-in procedures, and the requirement to have eight, ten, or more numbers and symbols in passwords does little to address these problems. It actually encourages people to behave irresponsibly, making it easier for hackers.

I can't remember how many times I have received "Error Message 404" or its equivalent. These are nonsensical codes used "to explain" whatever problem has occurred. They remind me of airlines attempting to justify flight delays. They make announcements in airports blaming them on weather, air traffic control problems, some other airliner not pulling away from its gate – anything that will deflect responsibility from themselves. One suspects these announcements are programmed by a random excuse generator. So it is in my story, where an airline attempts to pin the blame unfairly on one of their more responsible and capable employees.

The proliferation of passwords and the struggle with them is a quintessential problem of modernity. It is part and parcel of the bureaucratization of life. Fin de siècle German sociologist Max Weber identified bureaucracy as the dominant institutional feature of modernity. He regarded it as enabling but crippling. It made large organizations and governments possible. But in the name of efficiency, it imposed rules that were not only stifling to human creativity but by treating people as categories and numbers reduced them to objects. Rules, moreover, must be simple to be understood and are likely to be enforced in a heavy-handed way. They limit the authority and independence of individuals. In the face of changed circumstances the rules no longer make sense and end up a barrier to efficiency. Weber feared that ordinary citizens, would live in "a steel-hardened cage" of serfdom. He also worried that bureaucracy threatened to reorient people's loyalties by narrowing their horizons to those of their institution. In the absence of deeper ethical commitments, bureaucracy would impose its own values on people. The *Kulturmensch* [man of culture] would give way to the *Fachmensch* [occupational specialist]. For the latter, the only ethical yardstick would be the interests and power of the organization. Quoting Nietzsche, Weber predicted "the 'last men' would be "specialists without spirit [and] sensualists without heart."[8]

Weber attributed the downside of bureaucracy to the very rationality that made it so powerful and effective. For better and worse, it treated people alike and did its best to deprive them of their individuality. Franz Kafka also considered bureaucracy a defining feature of the modern age, but evaluated its consequences with an even more jaundiced eye. He emphasized bureaucracy's pathology, which he attributed to its lack of transparency and freedom from democratic oversight. For Weber, bureaucracy performs tasks in accordance with the law and directives from higher political authority. For Kafka, it is a law unto itself. It seeks to preserve and extend its power and buttress the authority and self-esteem of its officials. Bureaucracy succeeds in part by becoming opaque in its procedures and making its officials inaccessible to the public. Even those who work in the bureaucracy may understand little more than their assigned tasks and corner of the organization.[9] Password mania is a manifestation of this process. Passwords are designed to benefit the organization more than they are to serve and protect us and are imposed and managed in a way to make them increasingly self-defeating. It is another example of how many benefits of modernity were undercut by the procedures that accompany them.

"Physician, Heal Thyself" speaks to "Foo Fighters." Tony and his flight crew were mere numbers to army air force brass. Their accomplishments are measured in tons of ordnance dropped, not in targets destroyed. Crews were dispensable, in part because they were plentiful. With the help of statisticians, the army air force figured out how many missions they would have to fly before being rotated home. The army air force did their best to strike a fine balance between their goal of dropping bombs and ability to replace expected losses. They also had to maintain minimal morale to ensure that crew would go in the air and make serious efforts to hit their designated targets.

The principal reason losses were high is that the army air force flew during the day in contrast to the safer night-time missions flown by the British. They also went deeper into Germany, and this before they had effective fighter escorts with disposable fuel tanks. They flew these costlier missions primarily for organizational reasons; they were anxious to show how effective they were in destroying targets and thereby gain independence from the army and become a separate branch of the armed forces. Night-time bombing was notoriously inaccurate, and the generals relied on their new Norden bombsight – which could only function in daylight -- and heavily armed B-17s to achieve their goal. Bombing remained notoriously unreliable and attacks against heavily defended industrial sites were too costly to continue. The generals switched to city busting with the goal of killing people and destroying German morale. Neither strategy worked – the postwar bombing survey suggested that "strategic" bombing damaged oil and industrial production but strengthened civilian resolve -- but the army air force chose metrics that gave the appearance of success.[10] The lives of B-17 crews were put at risk or wasted for very little purpose.

The air force played the same game in Vietnam and the army relied on so-called "body counts" – how many Viet Cong and North Vietnamese soldiers they killed. As these numbers went up, they inspired confidence in the Pentagon and Defense Department. They were, of course, greatly exaggerated, and no measure of what was in essence a largely political struggle for influence.[11] As those on the ground in "Surviving Tet" recognized, their metrics blinded Washington to the uncomfortable truth that they were losing the war. Some argue for the more nefarious possibility that the generals knew this and stuck with their metrics as a form of denial or simply as a means of looking good in the eyes of the Johnson and then Nixon administrations.

"Foo Fighters" also has personal connections. Our row house in Rego Park, Queens was only a few miles from LaGuardia Airport. I was fascinated by airplanes and my father would use some of his precious gasoline ration to drive me to LaGuardia, which had become an important transit point for planes being sent to the European Theater of Operations. The pilots were women and the planes whatever was scheduled to cross the Atlantic. P-47 Thunderbolt and P-51 Mustang fighters and B-17 and B-24 bombers passed through. The airport was constantly expanding with temporary buildings of all kinds adjacent to its original Art Deco terminal and hangars. Parking was chaotic, with changing roadways, signs, and parking areas.

One Saturday, my cousin Steve joined us. My mother Ruth was a nervous and annoying back seat driver. She warned Dad not to turn where he was heading. He insisted that the dirt track led to a parking area, and for once Mom was right. We went around a hangar and discovered ourselves on an active taxi-way. Coming slowly toward us was a bomber and I shouted out that it was a B-24. This was not the question foremost in the mind of either parent. Dad had by now come to a halt, as did the bomber. The engines were feathered, a side door opened, and a woman in flight overalls and a leather helmet stuck out her head and shouted at the top of her lungs: "What the fuck are you doing here?" Steve and I learned our first four-letter word.

I knew the War was serious business. People were being killed. The Nazis were evil and had to be defeated. Following my parents and most Americans – and I felt very American by 1945 -- I had a black-and-white view of the War. We were the good guys, they – Germans, Japanese, and Italians – were the bad guys. Our bombers were the best, their crews the bravest and we would prevail. I devoured the news about Hiroshima and Nagasaki with pleasure, again taking my cue from grownups that these bombings would end the War and save American lives. The seeds of more critical inquiry were nevertheless sown. Our block had a high percentage of immigrants: Jews, non-Jewish Germans who were anti-Nazi, and anti-fascist Italians. They were all nice people and their kids were my friends. My solidarity with them clashed with efforts to demonize Axis peoples, especially Germans and Japanese. I remember wondering what it would be like to have Japanese neighbors and friends. Would they be any different?

My initial disillusionment with government was also war-related. Everyone on the "Home Front" was encouraged to recycle. I had a little red wagon with rubber wheels. I joined the other kids on the block to collect fats, tin cans, other kinds of meal, and newspapers, all for use in war production. One of my friend's dads took everything we gathered to a collection point. Sometime after the War I learned that people were so good about recycling that the government was overwhelmed and simply dumped much of what they received. So much for my effort to help win the War. I now used my wagon to carry around my collection of toy planes. The pride of my collection was wooden model B-17 that dad and I had assembled and that he carefully painted.

By the late 1940s I was devouring books about the War and especially the role of aircraft. I read about the fire-bombings of German and Japanese cities and, thanks to John Hersey, about the destruction wrought by the atom bombs dropped on Hiroshima and Nagasaki. We may have been the good guys but we did not always behave like them. To be sure, there were difficult trade-offs to be made between ethics and military advantage, but my reading indicated that these trade-offs were never framed as such. Almost everywhere, leaders did what they thought was advantageous – and all the more so if other people or peoples paid the price. As often as not, what they thought advantageous was not. The bombing of Germany and the atom bombing of Hiroshima and Nagasaki are cases in point. The invasions of Afghanistan and Iraq are more recent examples. Nothing much has changed.

"Gregor Samsa's Sister" was, of course, inspired by Kafka's famous "Metamorphosis." It lends itself to multiple interpretations. If one focuses on the reaction of Gregor Samsa's family to his becoming a giant insect it can be read as an extreme version of families confronted with problematic and embarrassing children because of their physical or mental handicaps or unacceptable behavior. We have all read about people giving away such children, putting them in institutions, or even hiding them in attics and cellars. The story can also be read from Gregor's perspective and his struggle to understand his new body and minimize the embarrassment and discomfort he has caused his family. Either approach sheds light on the problem of modernity and the constraining, if not dehumanizing, bourgeois values and life-style to which it has given rise.

I chose to tell the story from the perspective of Gregor's sister Greta. She is a talented and nubile young woman who is upwardly mobile and deeply attached to her family, especially her brother. Gregor's transformation has major consequences for her as it does for her family. If word gets out that her brother has become a giant insect Greta is at risk of losing her job, her suitor, and the musical career to which she aspires. She has hard choices to make as her interests and those of her brother and family appear to clash. My story is about her shifting commitment from her brother to herself. She is initially protective of him, but less so, Kafka suggests, as the crisis deepens. It is a universal tale about how hormones and ambition drive people and then offer justifications for what they have done.

Greta Samsa's dilemma is a fictional version of the kind of tragic choices that people and policymakers regularly confront. Greta is somewhat more self-aware than many political leaders but still tries to finesse any choice and then to deny she is making one when she does. She and her family have good defenses, no doubt in part because they support one another in their decision to abandon Gregor. As Kafka tells us, they go off at the end of the story for a picnic in the countryside.

The least unsettling part of Kafka's tale may be Gregor's transformation into an insect. It is such an unlikely, really impossible, event that we are not afraid of something similar happening to us. How our family responds to us is another matter. Healthy people generally come from healthy families where people stand by one another through thick and thin. The Samsas do not pass this test. Fear, economic, career, and love interests undermine family solidarity and reveal how shallow it is. This is even more true of social structures not based on blood ties. Kafka suggests that in the end we are alone in a generally cruel world. It is also a world filled with irony because a large part of what destroys the Samsas as a family is the search by individuals for belonging.

Kafka's tale and mine encourage readers to consider the counterfactual: what would have happened if the Samsas had responded differently to Gregor? He would presumably have survived his transformation although lost his job and the income on which the family was dependent. An innovative father or sister might have made some arrangement with a university or museum of natural history to use him as an object of study and receive some payment in return. They might not unreasonably have hoped that one day he would wake up his old self. Either way they would have kept him alive and managed to communicate with him as Kafka has Gregor retain his full mental capacities. At worst, he would have spent the remainder of his life in the apartment and have been treated as a member of the family.

Greta's fears of the social consequences to herself and her family of public knowledge of Gregor's condition are not unreasonable. They might well have been shunned by neighbors and it is certainly possible that Greta's beau would have looked elsewhere for female companionship. Nobody in the family seems to have thought the matter through and to have made any considered choices. Rather, they respond emotionally, and the predominant emotion for all of them is fear. For the parents the fear is literal and visceral fright when confronted with a large and "ugly" insect. For Greta it is fear in the Aristotelian sense; she imagines all kinds of future negative consequences for herself if word about her brother's condition becomes public. There is no evidence in Kafka's story, or mine, of careful risk assessment by the Samsa family. Their fright and fears propel them to act, in non-reflexive ways by the parents and in a calculating way by Greta. Both routes lead them to betray their son or brother.

"Rough Waters" is another tragic tale, and one with the usual mix of sympathetic and unsympathetic figures. The catalyst was the almost daily stories we read about the plight of political and economic refugees from Africa and the Middle East. There are enough drownings that the dangers of crossing the Mediterranean have become normalized in our minds. I attempt to create empathy by imaging a world in which we – or people very much like us – are the refugees. Aristotle thought the defining feature of tragedy was its *peripeteia* (reversal). This usually takes the form of a dramatic change in a hero's circumstances, the classic example being the fate of Oedipus. The tension of tragedy is enhanced by the audience's recognition that a reversal is about to occur well before the hero comes to this realization. Henry, Charlotte, and their daughters set out on their journey in high hopes of escaping the growing horrors of England and making a new life for themselves in Sub-Saharan Africa. We know that their flight will prove more perilous than they do, which creates tension that is not resolved until close to the end of the tale.

There is a more fundamental and dramatic *peripeteia* that drives the plot line. This is the gradual freezing of northern Europe brought about by climate change. It produces a dramatic reversal in living conditions in Europe and Africa, encouraging a reverse migration. This may seem far-fetched to some readers, but many scientists think this world is around the corner. The Gulf Stream has already slowed to a crawl and is in danger of stopping. If it does, the glaciers will return to northern Europe in short order. Henry and Charlotte are stand-ins for all of us and the reversal of fate the story describes is ours. Tragic heroes recognize what is in store for them too late to do anything about it. This is true of Henry and Charlotte, but not of humanity in general. There is still time to slow or stop climate change, but not much time, and dramatic action is required. It will not happen unless people demand changes from their governments, who otherwise will continue to do the bidding of corporations intent on making short-term profits at the expense of our well-being, if not the lives of our children and grandchildren.

Friends who read an early draft of this story liked it, but some suggested Henry and Charlotte were insufficiently anxious about their migration given the perils faced by refugees. I had deliberately refrained from imparting any real sense of terror or helplessness to them. They are Westerners, wealthy and educated in comparison to most African asylum seekers. They have a false sense of confidence and try to treat their adventure as something of a holiday.

Psychologists tell us that people find it difficult to make decisions that involve important trade-offs, as becoming a refugee certainly does. People try to postpone such decisions, which is why it takes something extraordinary to convince them to leave their homes and countries for an uncertain future. If they screw up their courage and commit themselves to a course of action that they recognize involves significant risks they are like to "spread the alternatives." They convince themselves that what initially appeared to be something like a 51 to 49 percent one is now a 90-10 choice. They become correspondingly insensitive to information and warnings that suggest their venture may prove fruitless or disastrous.[12] I imagine that many Syrian, Libyan, and other African refugees invoked psychological defenses of this kind to cope with the anxiety aroused by leaving home. The key here is the belief that the existing course of action – staying put – is unacceptable. People often find it easier to imagine the horrors that await them at home than they do those they may encounter on the road. The former can be more vivid to them, especially if horrible things have happened to friends or neighbors. Psychologists find that vividness is central to decisions of this kind.[13]

I have a great appreciation for the kinds of decisions refugees make, and the difficult choices they confront between known dangers at home and unknown ones on the road. My original family was rounded up in France in July of 1942 and for many years I thought I was the only survivor. I was hidden in a village, smuggled over the Pyrenees into Spain, crossed the U-boat infested Atlantic, entered the US as an illegal immigrant, was sent to an orphanage, adopted by a loving American family, and made a citizen by a sympathetic judge when my adoption became legal. The odds of my survival and good fortune were not high and every day I think about those who did not have my string of extraordinary breaks. It is in our power to do something about refugees. Small, hardly noticed, sacrifices by many people can have huge positive consequences for those at risk. The refugees in my story are compelled to search for a new life, and accept the risks involved by climate change. Here too, small sacrifices or minor good deeds can have profoundly beneficial effects in averting a looming and perhaps planet-wide disaster.

To make these sacrifices – and to feel good about making them – we have to get outside ourselves, or as Rousseau would suggest, inside ourselves, to discover our basic humanity. Either way, we must take a step back from our daily concerns, roles, and short-term interests to recognize how our fate – and that of our planet – is inextricably connected with others. This kind of reflection must be supplemented by empathy for others and the emotional satisfaction that develops from helping them. Reason and emotion combined can connect us with others, lead to more selfless behavior, and make us feel better about ourselves.

"Looking East" offers another variant of this dilemma. Lubec, Maine is a deeply divided town where traditional solidarity has been eroded by COVID and its politicization by Donald Trump and his Republican supporters. I dramatize this conflict in the escalating struggle between a MAGA hat wearing Trumpite who dismisses the virus as an invention of the Democrats and a liberal physician who is struggling to cope with a rising number of infections and the refusal of some – among them our protagonist – to wear masks, social distance, or get vaccinated.

Given its political divisions I thought Lubec the perfect setting for a Romeo and Juliet type tale where two young lovers – the daughter and son of the Trump supporter and the doctor -- confront hostility from their warring families. Karl Marx observed that when history repeats itself it is often a tragedy the first time around and a farce the second. Our young couple, who read Shakespeare's play in school contemplate a similar plot but in the expectation of a happier ending. They struggle – as I did – to come up with a scenario that is not too dangerous but also promises to compel their parents to put their conflict aside. Everything they and I could think up verged on the farcical, so the plot moved elsewhere.

The other problem was with my Trump supporter. He embodies all the evils xxiv Introduction

of the far-right and has the kind of authoritarian personality that makes him a bad husband and father. This is a credible portrayal of many of Trump's most vocal supporters but also made him too cardboard a character for my liking. So I decided to give Ron some nuance and the bastard changed before my eyes. He felt guilty about slapping his daughter when he learned that she was dating the son of his nemesis and that some peeping tom had posted on-line photos of them making out on the beach. His apology took the wind out of my plot. I got even by giving him COVID, which he deserved for not wearing a mask, getting vaccinated, and for going to the Sturgis, SD motorcycle rally, which, as predicted, was a super spreader. I struggled to portray him as having some admirable qualities but not doing any kind of incredible about-face. I leave it for readers to decide if I squared this circle successfully. Is it possible to be a Trump supporting, science denying, democrat-hating, conspiracy theorist and still have some kind of positive relationship with your family and respect for the independence of your wife and children?

"A Night at the Opera" is the other story that was previously published", although it appears here in revised form. It is an outgrowth of my research on counterfactuals -- "what ifs" in everyday English. Counterfactuals are, or should be, of great interest to social scientists interested in causation. If we posit that "X" caused "Y" we are also saying, other things being equal, in the absence of "X" there would be no "Y." To make a credible causal claim we must test this counterfactual case. Causation is, of course, never so simple, especially in the social world where events have multiple causes, and it is impossible to isolate hypothesized causes as we can sometimes do in the bench sciences.

When I wrote this story, I was tilting at the irrational belief held by many historians and social scientists that the past was "overdetermined" – that is more or less had to happen as it did – but that the future is wide open.[14] Past and future are, of course, logical equivalents, with the future becoming the past in due course – and more rapidly so at my age. The events seen as most determined by most people are those closest to the present. The further back we go, the more contingent they appear. People will see the COVID pandemic and the 9.11 attacks more difficult to have forestalled than, say

---

** Richard Ned Lebow, *Forbidden Fruit: Counterfactuals and International Relations* (Princeton: Princeton University Press, 2010), ch. 7.

World War I or Lincoln's assassination regardless of the merit of the case. They will be more resistant to counterfactuals that unmake recent events than those that undo more distant events. However, the more vivid we make our counterfactuals the more credible they become to those exposed to them. Vividness in this context means making the story come alive by adding details that make it easier for readers to put themselves into the tale.

A former colleague and I conducted an experiment in which we "unpacked" alternative endings to the Cuban missile crisis. We told the same story about a different outcome three times but on each occasion added more detail. The first scenario gave three other possible outcomes for the crisis. The second added three reasons for each of these outcomes. The final scenario added irrelevant details such as the weather and names of ships. Detail made each account more vivid and more credible to the historians, international relations scholars, and policymakers in our sample.

In a follow-on experiment I tried to get vividness to work in reverse, that is to make a counterfactual scenario less plausible. I devised what I called a "long-shot" counterfactual to prevent World War I. Such counterfactuals involve multiple, minimal rewrites of history at some temporal distance from the event they are intended to mutate. They generally require a longer and elaborate chain of logic linking them to the event in question. They also need enabling counterfactuals to sustain their chain of logic. Although people see events as more contingent the further back from them in time one asks, I hypothesized that long-shot counterfactuals should be judged less credible than their close-call counterparts because of their longer chain of logic and greater number of enabling counterfactuals. I further surmised that their plausibility will be affected negatively by their vividness, an attribute that is otherwise assumed to enhance the plausibility of counterfactuals. The experimental results confirm this proposition.

"A Night at the Opera" was the instrument for my experiment. It is a short story set in a counterfactual world where there was no First World War nor anything like it. My heroine imagines how different this world might have been if Mozart had died at 35, the age of her partner. She constructs a chain of logic leading from the great Austrian composer's premature death to a conflagration in 1914. The argument rests on the political effects of Romanticism and how it would have flourished if Mozart had died young. This account is followed by a blistering critique from an imaginary reviewer for a journal to whom the story has been submitted. The critic uses standard social science arguments to show why our world could not possibly exist! A short, third part of the story is an angry rejoinder by my heroine.

The three-part tale is, of course, tongue in cheek. It is intended to be amusing, but also to raise seriously the prospect that small, seemingly insignificant developments in domains far removed from international relations might nevertheless have profound political consequences. This flies in the face of common sense in two ways: we don't expect music or poetry to shape politics, and we think big developments must have big causes. In my experiment I asked a control group of historians, international relations scholars, and policymakers to assess the contingency of World War I or anything like it in the second decade of the twentieth century. The experimental group was asked the same question – but only after reading the first part of the story, where the heroine in effect untracks World War I by means of Mozart's longevity. The international relations scholars and historians in the experimental group evaluated the contingency of World War I significantly lower than the control group.

The variation in this and related experiments supports the general understanding in the psychological literature that causation should be understood as a distinctly perceptual category.[15] It also indicates that historians, international relations scholars, and people in the policy world combine an interesting mix of political sophistication and cognitive naiveté. They have no difficulty recognizing the implications of counterfactuals and are strongly motivated to accept or reject them on the basis of their world views. Participants can nevertheless be encouraged by means of counterfactual priming to acknowledge more contingency that they otherwise would. "Psychologic" has the potential to render their judgments logically incoherent. This is most evident in the case of long-shot counterfactuals, which can reduce overall judgments of contingency by historians and international relations scholars despite surveys across cases that indicate that they judge events and outcomes increasingly contingent the further back in time from an event they are asked to make these assessments. These contradictions between beliefs and assessments might be reconciled with reference to the effects of vividness on estimates of contingency, but this in turn raises further questions about the ways in which scholars make assessments of historical contingency.

My experiments dramatize the tension between "psycho-logic" and the laws of statistical inference, which guide the imaginary critique. Psycho-logic describes the various cognitive and motivational biases that make estimates of probability and attributions of responsibility different from the expectations of so-called rational models. Biases and heuristics of all kinds can and have been described and documented by standard psychological studies and case studies of political decision making. Understanding biases intellectually and "feeling" them emotionally are not the same thing. The latter, I contend, is essential if we are to free ourselves from their grip. It is equally important to understand the conservative bias of the laws of statistical inference to avoid becoming their unwitting prisoner. Psycho-logic, which makes us more receptive to contingency by reason of the vividness of its narratives, is one way of preventing this.

My story has relevance to fiction more generally. Good stories are vivid stories. We empathize with their characters and the circumstances they confront – or are repelled by them. We respond emotionally, not just reflexively. Our vicarious experience of others' suffering, as Aristotle maintained in the case of tragedy, can have profound consequences for how we understand ourselves and the world. For this reason, novels like Goethe's *The Sorrows of Young Werther (1774)*, and Harriet Becher Stowe's *Uncle Tom's Cabin (1852)*, John Steinbeck's *Grapes of Wrath (1939)*, and George Orwell's *1984 (1948)* have had profound social or political influence. Fiction that people take for fact, as with conspiracy theories, can also have profound real-world consequences. Entering fictional worlds can thus have divergent effects, and this is where reflection and caution come into play. But reflection is also a double-edged sword. It is beneficial when it makes us question dubious claims but not when our pre-conceptions imprison us. Literature performs a service not only when it connects us with other people but opens our minds to their perspectives.

REFERENCES

1   At around the same time as my interview Kissinger told Hans J. Morgenthau that "in 1965 when I first visited Vietnam, I became convinced that what we were doing there was hopeless. I decided to work within the government to get the war ended." Jeremy Suri, *Henry Kissinger and the American Century* (Cambridge: Harvard University Press, 2009), p. 188.

2   Richard Ned Lebow, *The Tragic Vision of Politics: Interests, Orders, and Ethics* (Cambridge: Cambridge University Press, 2003).

3   Ibid.

4   Charles M. Blow, "Ron DeSantis, How Many Covid Deaths Are Enough?" *New York Times*, 29 August 2021, https://www.nytimes.com/2021/08/29/opinion/ron-desantis-covid-death.html (accessed 29 August 2021).

5   Wikipedia, "List of conspiracy theories propagated by Donald Trump," 16 August 2021, https://en.wikipedia.org/wiki/List_of_conspiracy_theories_promoted_by_Donald_Trump (accessed 31 August 2021).

6   On this subject, see Matthew Evangelista and Henry Shue, eds., *The American Way of Bombing: Changing Ethical and Legal Norms, from Flying Fortresses to Drones* (Ithaca: Cornell University Press, 2014).

7   Frederick Taylor, *Dresden: Tuesday, 13 February 1945* (New York: HarperCollins, 2004), p. 42.

8   Max Weber, *The Protestant Ethic and the Spirit of Capitalism*, trans. Stephen Kalberg (Oxford: Oxford University Press, 2011), p. 178, quoting Friedrich Nietzsche, Ecce Homo.

9   Franz Kafka, "The Judgment," in Kafka, *Complete Stories*, (New York: Schocken Books, 1972), pp. 77-88, "The Metamorphosis," in Kafka, *Complete Stories*, pp. 89-139, *The Castle*, trans. Mark Harnan (New York: Schocken Books, 1998), and *The Trial*, trans. Breon Mitchell (New York: Schocken Books, 1998). For a comparison, Richard Ned Lebow, *Reason and Cause: Social Science in a Social World* (Cambridge: Cambridge University Press, 2021), ch. 7.

10 United States Strategic Bombing Survey, Summary Report, European War, 30 September 1945, Department of War, https://www.anesi.com/ussbs02.htm (accessed 7 September 2021).

11 Scott Sigmund Gardner and Marissa Edson Myers, "Body Counts and

"Success" in the Korean and Vietnam Wars," *Journal of Interdisciplinary History 25, no. 3* (1995), pp. 377-95; Marilyn B. Young, *Body and Nation* (Durham, N. C.: Duke University Press, 2014), ch. 11.

12 The classic work on this subject is Irving Janis, and Leon Mann, *Decision Making: A Psychological Analysis of Conflict, Choice, and Commitment.* New York: Free Press, 1977).

13 L. Ross, M. R. Lepper, F. Strack and J. Steinmetz, "Social Explanation and Social Expectation: Effects of Real and Hypothetical Explanations on Subjective Likelihood," *Journal of Personality and Social Psychology* 35, no. 11 (1977), pp. 817-29; Amos Tversky and Daniel Kahneman, "Extensional versus Intuitive Reason: The Conjunction Fallacy as Probability Judgment," *Psychological Review* 90, no. 2 (1983), pp. 292-315; Philip Tetlock, and Richard Ned Lebow "Poking Counterfactual Holes in Covering Laws: Cognitive Styles and Political Learning," *American Political Science Review* 95, no. 4 (2001), pp. 829-43; Richard Ned Lebow, "Scholars and Causation 2," in Richard Ned Lebow, *Forbidden Fruit: Counterfactuals and International Relations* (Princeton; Princeton University Press, 2010), pp. 166-95.

14 On this belief, see Baruch Fischoff, "Hindsight is not Equal to Foresight: The Effect of Outcome Knowledge on Judgment under Uncertainty," *Journal of Experimental Psychology: Human Perception and Performance* 1, no. 2 (1975), pp. 288-99; S. A. Hawkins and R. Hastie, "Hindsight: Biased Judgments of Past Events after the Outcomes are Known," Psychological Bulletin 107, no. 3 (1990), pp. 311-27.

15 Fritz Heider and Marianne Simmel, "An Experimental Study of Apparent Behavior," *American Journal of Psychology,* 57 (1944), pp. 243-59; A. E. Michotte, *La perception de la causalité* (Louvain: University of Louvain Publications, 1946); Daniel Kahneman, "Varieties of Counterfactual Thinking," in Neal J. Roese and James M. Olson, eds., *What Might Have Been: The Social Psychology of Counterfactual Thinking* (Mahwah, N.J.: Erlbaum, 1995), pp. 375-96.

NIXON IN HELL

Hell was nothing like Richard Nixon thought it would be, not that he had thought much about it when he was "upside." That was the term everyone here used to describe the world in which they had once lived. It was an ironic reference to the ancient and erroneous belief that Hell was subterranean. As far as anyone could figure out, it wasn't anywhere in relation to earth. But in every other way it was undeniably the "downside," so the term stuck.

On the few occasions that Nixon had thought about Hell, usually during interminable church services that presidents feel compelled to attend, he imagined fire and brimstone and little red devils with spears and evil grins, swishing their tails in delight when they made tortured souls writhe in agony. Hell may once have been like that , opinion among "lifers" was divided. but over the centuries it had evolved to reflect lessons the devil and his assistants had learned from observing life on earth. Not that they lacked imagination, but when it came to torture, human beings showed an ingenuity and dedication that the devil found inspiring. So Hell was frequently remodeled to take advantage of the latest in human innovation. Some time back, the devil had installed an ornate, wrought iron gate with the words *Arbeit macht frei* [work makes you free] across the top. Scuttlebutt had it that his assistants were now upgrading modules to incorporate the latest in computer graphics technology. Virtual torture would free more assistants for administrative tasks, always a crushing burden in eras of extraordinary growth.

Nixon entered Hell through the devil's gate, and being a well-read man, understood its significance all too well. Inside, he caught sight of a devil -- he looked like everyone else, but his tail gave him away. He was dressed in a smartly tailored S.S. uniform and barking out orders to *Kapos* -- prisoners who worked for the camp authorities in return for special privileges. They used their bull whips to separate terrified newcomers into two groups and herd them off in different directions. Nixon and about twenty other souls were marched off through the mud to one of the hundreds of squat, wooden barracks that formed a grid on the seemingly endless plain. The sky was gray and the fast moving, low clouds gave the camp something of a two-dimensional quality. Dressed in a tropical weight suit Nixon began to shiver.

The barracks smelled something fierce, but they were at least warm. They were largely deserted; Nixon wondered if their prior occupants had been gassed. The S.S. guard escorting them shouted something in German that Nixon did not understand. An old man, lying on one of the bottom bunks, looked up and explained in heavily accented English that Nixon was expected to undress and change into one of the blue and white striped uniforms stacked in two neat piles in a corner of the barracks. Nixon looked around and saw a few of his group beginning to shed their clothes. He had always been uncomfortable about undressing in front of other people, and in his student days had usually managed to find some ruse to avoid changing in locker rooms. The whip exploded in the air in front of Nixon's face, and he involuntarily jumped back in fright. The guard shouted at him, and Nixon took off his jacket and fumbled with his tie.

The two-piece uniform was stiff and uncomfortable, but had been freshly laundered. The pants were too tight, and the jacket was at least two sizes too large. The contrast with his argyle socks and soft leather, Italian shoes was striking. The old man told him that the bunk above his was unoccupied, and that he should take it. To Nixon, all the bunks looked unoccupied, but then he realized that nobody came here with luggage or personal effects. He wondered how he would brush his teeth; he looked around and noticed there was no sink.

"Where do I wash up?" he asked.

The old man smiled. "You don't."

"What did I do to deserve this? I'm not a Jew! Why have they sent me here? There must have been a mistake. . . unless one of those [expletive deleted] reporters was responsible for this."

"Relax," the old man said. "Nobody here is Jewish or Gypsy. Beelzebub is sadistic but not insensitive."

"Or else he has a wicked sense of humor," volunteered another man.

Nixon turned to address him. "What do you mean?"

"Think about it," he said. "No Jews or Romany, but a permanent work force of former guards or petty officials at Nazi concentration camps, or people somehow connected with Hitler's campaigns of extermination. They are treated like shit, and there's no hope of liberation." He shook his head. "Endless cycles of hard labor and beatings. Freezing in the winter, roasting in the summer."

"I'd slit my throat," Nixon volunteered.

"You can't," the second man said. That's the beauty of it. Nobody dies here, because you're already dead! There's no way out unless they ship you off somewhere."

Nixon's voice grew animated. "You mean some people leave here alive?"

"Alive? Let's not get into that one. But yes, people, most of them, leave. The place looks like Auschwitz-Birkenau, but it is a processing center, not a death camp. Most new arrivals stay here no longer than a week or two. They get shipped out in cattle cars to other locations for resettlement."

Nixon gave him a quizzical look. "So it's Auschwitz in reverse?"

"More or less. It's a devilishly clever scheme, don't you agree?"

The conversation was interrupted by the return of the other inhabitants of the barracks. They passed through the door one at a time, trudged across its floor of bare wooden planking and sought out their bunks in silence. Nixon looked at them in horror.

"It's O.K.," said the old man reading his thoughts. They're not Nazis, just ordinary sinners like you and me."

"Ordinary sinners, you say?"

"Run-of-the-mill mass murderers."

"Murderers? I'm not a murderer!"

The door opened again and a detail of *Kapos* pushed through a wheelbarrow that contained two large, covered, metal cauldrons. Inmates rose from their bunks, grabbed their tin bowls and quickly lined up to be served a thin gruel and chunks of stale, pale, gray-colored bread. Nixon was hungry but revolted by the smell of the gruel and could not bring himself to go through the chow line. He stood in front of his bunk thinking about suppers on his terrace overlooking the Pacific. "What I wouldn't give for a bowl of cottage cheese and ketchup!" he said to himself.

The old man consumed his gruel with enthusiasm and used a piece of bread to soak up whatever liquid was left in the bottom of his bowl. Nixon watched him in amazement. Just like an animal, he thought. The old man popped the last piece of bread into his mouth and replaced his empty bowl on a nail sticking out from the side of his bunk. Nixon waited from him to get into his bunk before resuming their conversation.

"You said this is a camp for mass murderers?"

"That's right. Everyone here is guilty of it in some way, directly or indirectly. I could have saved Jews during the Holocaust. The man who spoke to you earlier helped to plan the fire- bombing of Tokyo. Jean-Claude over there wiped out villages during the Algerian war of independence. Hami killed French settlers." The old man pointed to the bunk above Jean-Claude. "They're inseparable buddies."

"I didn't kill anybody!"

"Nobody wants to think of himself as a murderer."

A *Kapo* arrived with a footstool and positioned it under one of four naked bulbs that provided illumination to the windowless barracks. He had to unscrew each bulb from its socket; they were very hot, and he could only give them a quick twist before removing his hand. It took five or six tries before the first bulb flickered and went out. The *Kapo* blew on his fingers to ease the pain before moving the stool into position under the next bulb. When the barracks was dark, the *Kapo* left, and Nixon heard the sound of a padlock being attached to the door.

"They lock us in for the night?" he asked the old man.

"Yes, not that there's anywhere to go."

"What if I have to go to the bathroom? I have a weak bladder."

"You'd better learn to control it."

"There's no john in the barracks?"

"I think you should go to bed," the old man said.

Nixon gingerly raised his foot and put it on the wooden frame of the old man's bunk to get a better purchase on his own bunk. He grabbed the sideboard above and tried twice without success to pull himself up. He waited to catch his breath before trying again.

The old man suggested that he grab one end of the frame and hook his leg over the other end. "Then you should be able to pull yourself up and roll over on to the mattress."

"Maybe I'll just sleep on the floor."

"Go ahead. . . if you don't mind the rats."

Nixon thought about this for a minute, and decided to give it one more try. He followed the old man's instructions and after some effort made it into the bunk. He eased his tired body on to the lumpy, straw-filled mattress. There was no pillow.

The days that followed were miserable. Nixon was infested with lice and fleas, and scratching his bites only made them itch more. He ate nothing for two days and tried to ignore his hunger pangs. On the third day, cramps and severe stomach pains forced him into the chow line. He had been assigned to a work team that dug holes for the foundations of new barracks. It was back-breaking work, especially for somebody who was out of shape and suffered from phlebitis. After his first fifteen minutes of digging, he thought he was going to faint. He let his shovel drop and tried to steady himself while gasping for air. One of the *Kapo*s in charge of the work detail, a round-faced Asian, shouted at him in a language Nixon thought might be Chinese. He understood that he was supposed to resume work, but he was unable to move. The *Kapo* addressed him again and then lashed out with his coiled whip. Nixon felt its leather tip draw across his buttocks and was then overcome by an intense burning sensation. Somehow, his body found the energy to bend down to pick up the shovel.

Nixon struggled to come to terms with his situation. At first, he hoped it was just a particularly vivid nightmare. He gave that idea up after being abruptly awakened from a real dream the next morning by a *Kapo* marching through the barracks shaking a cow bell. He was mustered out of his bunk and the barracks and marched to the common latrine and showers. No dream, he decided, could have a smell so ugly and penetrating.

Nixon's next response was anger. The devil had no right to punish him this way. He was not a mass murderer; character assassination was his biggest sin. If he was here, where were Kennedy and Johnson? Those two were real criminals, he reassured himself. Kennedy had stolen the White House from him in 1960 by having the Daley machine stuff all those ballot boxes in Cook County. He was a fool for persuading his supporters that it was not in the national interest to challenge the election in the courts. And that egomaniac Johnson dragged the country into a useless war in Vietnam. It took him and Henry four years to get out with honor, and we would have done it sooner too if it those [expletive deleted] Democrats hadn't stirred up the hippies and tried to block their every move in Congress. Nixon began to think that Kennedy had bested him again. He had carefully cultivated his relationship with Billy Graham, but the Kennedy clan had all those cardinals eating out of their hands, even the Vatican, for all he knew. Maybe they got the pope to pull strings to send him here? Just the kind of thing they would do!

Nixon was also unhappy about the way he was being treated in Hell. Maybe he was a sinner, although assuredly not a murderer, but he was also a VIP. Nobody had met him at the gate, not that he expected old Lucifer himself. But the devil could have sent a couple of his assistants. Brezhnev must be here, Mao too. The thought was strangely comforting. He would have to ask them what kind of reception they had received. He wondered how they were holding up; he had difficulty imagining either of them digging ditches. For the first time since he had entered Hell, Nixon broke into a grin.

The old man with the Italian accent aside, nobody had briefed him about Hell. That would have been one of the perks of VIP treatment. He allowed himself to remember how attentive, well-dressed assistants and officers in crew cuts and perfectly pressed uniforms had fawned over him, anxiously soliciting his approval for memos, schedules and itineraries, even what to serve at state dinners. In Hell he was anonymous and powerless. Nobody deferred to him or told him anything, unless it was an order, and then it was usually barked in German or Chinese. Once Nixon had screwed up his courage to talk back. He had demanded that the *Kapo* marching his group off to a work site take him to see whoever was in charge. The *Kapo* told him to shut up, or so Nixon assumed from his tone of voice, but he continued to insist that he speak to someone in authority. The *Kapo* shrugged his shoulders and summoned a colleague to take over the work detail. He led Nixon off in a different direction to a small hut at some distance from any of the barracks. Nixon rehearsed the speech he would make, but he never got the chance. Two *Kapo*s appeared from nowhere with and began to beat him with rubber hoses. Nixon remembered absorbing a number of painful blows before losing consciousness.

After his beating, Nixon withdrew from camp life as much as possible and sought refuge in memories of pleasant upside moments. He went through the motions of morning ablution, work, meals, free time until he found release in sleep. His social interactions were limited to perfunctory conversations with the old man. Inner exile helped Nixon to preserve his dignity, and he almost convinced himself that reality was his mental reveries, not servitude in a concentration camp. Every afternoon when his work detailed finished, Nixon always managed to lead the procession back to the barracks. He would walk smartly up the steps and nod his head ever so slightly in acknowledgment to an imaginary band leader who struck up "Hail to the Chief" as soon as the president came into view.

Nixon's coping strategy was ultimately defeated by curiosity. He had an alert and inquiring mind that could only be suppressed for so long. It surreptitiously stored and processed information from his new environment, awaiting a propitious moment to intrude on his inner self. Nixon was vaguely aware that part of his mind was insubordinate and impossible to fully control. He gave this corner of his mind the nickname "Henry," and chose to tolerate it as long as it did not interfere with his fantasy life. This uneasy accommodation lasted for some time; Nixon really did not know for how long, nor did he care. Time's arrow was a tool used by the mind to order memories and expectations to cope with the world that Nixon had rejected.

He was brought back to reality by recognition of a familiar face. He had been digging an irrigation trench alongside a newly constructed barracks when another work detail passed by struggling to push wheelbarrows laden with bags of cement across the damp and uneven ground. The high-pitched scraping sounds of the wheels was as penetrating as it was

unpleasant, and Nixon involuntarily looked up to identify the source of
the annoyance. His subconscious mind registered the scene and the face of
the *Kapo* hurrying the work detail along and filed it away for subsequent
analysis. Later that afternoon Nixon was resting in his bunk having just
finished a long replay of the banquet Mao Zedong had held in his honor in
the Great Hall of the People. He had not enjoyed the food -- too much spice
and too many vegetables -- but he reveled in being the center of attention,
not only of Mao, but of the entire world. He was especially pleased that
Mao had directed most of his questions about America to him rather than
to Henry, and that this had been picked up by the press.

Nixon's mind went blank while his memory banks uploaded scenes from
his favorite film, *Around the World in Eighty Days*. His subconscious chose
this moment to intervene, and signaled Nixon that it had sighted someone
he knew. Nixon summoned up the image of the work detail in preference
to the movie. The *Kapo*'s face was indeed familiar, but he could not put a
name to it. He had never been good at recalling names, and it was always
more difficult to do so when he encountered people out of context. Nixon
wondered if anyone would recognize him. He had grown leaner, and as far
as he could tell -- there was no mirror in the barracks -- he had lost most of
his double chin. For some reason, neither his hair nor nails had grown, and
he pulled his fingers across his cheek to confirm that his skin was smooth
and lacking his tell-tale afternoon stubble. For the next hour or so he played
over the scene in his mind's eye. The long, angular face with deep-set eyes
was definitely somebody he knew from his political past, when they were
both much younger, he thought. It bothered him that he could not identify
the man, and decided to do what he could to arrange another encounter.

To do this, Nixon had to take a more active interest in camp life and began
to engage the old man in more animated discussion.

"I was worried about you," the old man confided.

"About me?" Nixon asked.

"Yes. A lot of people never come out of withdrawal. They don't want to
face the truth."

"What truth?"

"You need to find the answer to that yourself, my son."

Nixon began to wonder if he was the only sane person in the barracks. He absent-mindedly plucked a louse from beneath his shirt and calmly crushed it between his fingers. "How long have you been here old man?"

"Not very long. Twenty or thirty years. I don't rightly know."

"You don't know?"

"No. It's not important."

Nixon pondered his answer and decided not to pursue the line of questioning any further in the expectation that he would find any clarification even more depressing. Instead, he guided the conversation toward the camp and the work detail he had witnessed that morning. He learned that it contained upwards of 50,000 souls, who provided the labor force used to maintain and expand the camp. Ever since he had arrived, the old man explained, expansion had been underway, and there were rumors that this was only one of many concentration camps.

Nixon still hoped he might be one of the fortunate people in transit. Where would they send him? He remembered a newspaper column by that bastard Buchwald that proposed he be sentenced to an eternity in high school as punishment for Watergate. That would be just fine, he thought. There would be no back-breaking labor in high school, but recesses and hot school lunches. He salivated at the thought of the latter. Were there still hot lunches, or was it one of the programs his administration had cut? Nixon felt an unusual pang of guilt.

The old man interrupted Nixon's reverie. "If you were in transit, you would have been out of here already. You're one of us."

"What do you mean, one of us?"

"I told you when you first arrived. Everyone here is guilty in some way of mass murder."

"Now let me say this about that. . . ."

The old man raised his hand with an air of practiced authority and Nixon stopped in mid-sentence.

"As far as I can tell," the old man explained in a detached voice, "we have been divided into three groups. The largest number of people are those who abetted mass murder indirectly. They are people like Lou, who knew at the time it was wrong to calculate the distribution of incendiaries most likely to create a massive firestorm over Tokyo. Or, Hwang-ho, who, for a small bribe, told the Chinese authorities where anti-communist refugees were hiding. They were all slaughtered. There's even the odd spy who sold or gave away secrets that led to people's deaths. They work as laborers or do chores around the camp, like serving food and doing laundry."

"Laundry," Nixon said. "I've been in these clothes since I arrived. They're absolutely filthy!"

"*Piano, piano,*" the old man said, using his mother tongue with Nixon for the first time. "Everything here takes time, and you have lots of it before you."

At a loss for words, Nixon looked down at his feet. His favorite shoes were all but unrecognizable. If only he had known, he would have been buried in Gore-Tex hiking boots. The Egyptians had the right idea, he thought. They buried their dead with everything they were expected to need in the afterlife, although sandals would not last long here. He wondered why he had seen no Egyptians; everybody here was modern, although they came from every corner of the globe. In due course, he would have to ask the old man.

"Some people ultimately leave; where they go, I don't know." The old man made the sign of the cross. "The second group consists of people who actually committed atrocities. They do hard labor; I explained that to you earlier. The third group are the most serious offenders. They ordered or planned mass murder, or, like me, were in a position to stop it at little risk to themselves and failed to do so. They spend some time as *Kapos*, and are compelled to beat and torture other inmates."

"What sort of punishment is that?" Nixon asked.

"Think about it," the old man suggested. "For the most part these are people who see themselves, or used to anyway, as decent, even god-fearing folk. Many of them were caring parents, respectful of their neighbors and invariably kind to their pets. Did you ever notice that people are on the whole kinder to animals than they are to each other? Even when we slaughter animals for food, we try to do it as quickly and painlessly as possible."

"There are animal activists who would disagree," Nixon suggested.

"I know. There are people here who killed people to protect animals. Also people who killed to prevent abortion."

"You were telling me about punishment," Nixon reminded the old man.

"You're right, I digress. But there's really no reason to hurry. Some mass murderers are sadists. But many of the people responsible for mass murder are not, and pride themselves on having led exemplary lives. The violence they committed was never first-hand, so it was easy for them to deny responsibility. To the extent they thought about it, they convinced themselves they were merely cogs in the wheel or, if they were near to the apex of authority, that their behavior was compelled by reasons of state."

"It often is."

The old man ignored Nixon's comment. "Here in Hell, they get the opportunity to experience violence first-hand."

"I know. I've been beaten."

"No, you still don't understand. You get to beat people."

"What do you mean?" Nixon asked.

"In due course, they'll teach you to beat and torture people without doing too much damage to their internal organs. Just like medical school, you practice on dummies before you do it to real people."

"You're kidding!"

"I never joke," the old man said. "I wish I could. I think I would have had a happier life."

"I'm not known for my sense of humor either."

The old man lowered his voice, not that anybody was listening. "You get to beat other inmates, usually with truncheons or rubber hoses, but sometimes with your bare fists."

"I couldn't do that."

"Oh yes, you can," the old man insisted. "You will not only pummel people but burn them with cigarettes and shock them with cattle prods and metal clamps you attach to their nipples and testicles."

"I'll refuse!"

The old man shook his head and regarded Nixon with a look of pity. "It won't work. I said no at first. They frog-marched me to the outskirts of the camp and forced me into a hole just wide enough to accommodate me standing up. They kept me there for two days, without food or water, while water seeped in up to the level of my knees. I was still recalcitrant, so they thrashed me. I held out until they explained how they were going to force a glass catheter up my urethra and then manhandle my penis so that the catheter splintered into numerous fragments. They said the pain would be excruciating for years to come whenever I urinated."

Nixon shuddered and tried to push from his mind the image of a glass tube being rammed up his penis. He wouldn't even wish such a fate on the owners and staff of the *Washington Post*. The old man shook his head. "I even lack the courage to be a martyr. So I agreed to do what they wanted. At first it wasn't too awful. I worked over some newcomers with hoses. I tried not to hit them too hard, but the *Kapos* saw that I was holding back and threatened me with the catheter unless I lashed out with all my strength. It was awful. I beat the victims into unconsciousness."

"I know what that feels like," Nixon said.

"Believe me, it's pretty terrible on the giving end too. I thought they would let me go after a few beatings, but it only got worse. Each time I was pushed into doing something worse. They made me do unspeakable things." The old man crossed himself again.

"How long did this go on?"

"I don't know. In the end, they had me garrote a young man until his face turned blue and he collapsed. They told me I had killed him."

Nixon frowned. "I thought you said nobody died here?"

The old man shrugged his shoulders. "Every night I see his contorted face with his tongue sticking out and hear the gurgling sound he made as he struggled unsuccessfully to draw in air. Now I know what it means to be a murderer."

Hard labor, simple food and the absence of coffee and alcohol had worked wonders for Nixon's body. He had lost weight and his blood circulation had improved. He had also became increasingly inured to the fleas and lice that colonized his mattress and hair, and rarely bothered to scratch his bites. That night, Nixon lay awake in his bunk -- into which he now easily climbed -- thinking about what the old man had told him. He did not want to torture anybody, and he certainly did not want it done to him.

The next morning Nixon gave a perfunctory hello to the old man, and was relieved to throw himself into the numbing mindlessness of hard, physical labor. The work went quickly, and Nixon was not the least perturbed by the rain that splattered him during a brief late morning shower. He wondered if the devil was able to control the weather. The winter season was perennially gray with only rare glimpses of the sun. It rained or snowed almost every day; never enough to make work impossible, but enough to keep the ground wet and muddy and make work difficult. Nixon kept a sharp lookout for the *Kapo* he had seen the day before. He was absolutely certain it was somebody he knew.

When Nixon returned to the barracks, he found the old man lying in his bunk and anxious to resume their conversation. He decided to do his best to keep it away from the topic of the previous evening. The old man must have sensed his anxiety, and to Nixon's relief, talked about his adjustment to the routine of Hell.

"Most of the men here miss women," he told Nixon. But I've never been troubled by their absence in the camp. I was a priest and celibate even when I was young."

"I don't miss women either. But I do miss my wife. She did a good job of looking after me and never judged me. I'm glad she's not here. I wouldn't want her to see me now."

"What do you miss?

"Music. Music and books. I played the piano. I wasn't great, but I played well enough to enjoy it, show tunes and the like. Life -- or whatever this is

-- is going to be Hell without music."

"Nietzsche said there is no life without music." The old man reached up with his right hand to scratch his bald pate. "Little did he know."

"I had no idea Nietzsche said anything like that. I always thought of him as one of those nihilists."

"Well, there is that side of him," the old man conceded.

"Damn . . . . " Nixon stopped himself. "I probably shouldn't say that here."

The old man chuckled. "I don't think it can do you any harm."

"What I meant to say, is that I may have an eternity in front of me without music and books. I might enjoy reading Nietzsche, and certainly all the history and literature I never had time for upside. I'd give anything for a good book. . . especially if it were printed in large type."

"Don't be so sure," the old man said. He turned his back on Nixon and reached around and behind his mattress to pull out a bible. Nixon could tell immediately what it was from the gold cross embossed on the black, pseudo-leather cover.

The old man held it out to Nixon to inspect. "They gave me this a couple of days before they took me off for torture training."

Nixon took the bible and stared at it for several seconds. He wiped one hand and then the other on the cleanest part of his pants before fingering its pages. It would not have been his first choice of books, but he was overjoyed to see any book, a sign of the life he once knew. Tears welled up in his eyes.

"May I read it?"

"Of course. How could a priest refuse anyone a bible? Just be furtive about it. I don't know how the *Kapos* would respond if they caught you with it. You'd better stash it under your mattress."

"What about you? Don't you want to read it?"

"Not really. It's another one of the devil's little jokes."

"I don't understand."

The old man swallowed hard and scrunched up his leathery face. "I was a priest. I rose to a position of high authority in the church during difficult times. Secularism and materialism were luring people away from the faith, and much of Europe fell into the hands of two godless regimes that had declared war on Christianity. Italy was occupied by the Germans in September 1943, and the Bolsheviks were advancing daily in the East. The Church had no choice but to reach some accommodation with the Germans, and I also thought them the lesser of the two evils."

"Statesmanship requires compromise," Nixon said.

"I went too far. In looking after the interests of the Church I lost sight of the principles on which it was based." The old man paused, and Nixon stood silently shifting his weight from foot to foot waiting to see if he would continue.

The old man braced himself against the bunk frame and resumed his story. "Not long after the Germans occupied Rome the order came from Berlin to round up and deport the city's Jews. Many of them sought refuge in the Vatican, and I only allowed in those who had converted to Christianity, had a Christian parent or were somehow well-connected or otherwise useful. In October the S.S. put 1,007 Jews on a train destined for here, for Auschwitz-Birkenau. Two of my associates pleaded with me to join them and stand in front of the train in our robes and mitres in protest. They insisted that the Nazis would never dare move the train in our presence, and that our action would galvanize opposition to them all over Italy. I said no, and forbade them to take any action by themselves. I made only the weakest protest to the German ambassador. I later learned that the S.S. had orders to back off from any deportations if the Vatican expressed any serious opposition. All the people on the train died, and some of them were only children."

The old man crossed himself.

"You can see why I don't want to look at the bible, let alone read it. All it does it remind me of my moral failings. Perhaps one day when I have come to terms with my guilt. I will be able to take solace in the good book again."

Nixon realized that he was still holding the bible, and not wanting to give his friend any offence, reached over to stash it under his mattress. He noticed several bed bugs jump when he lifted up the corner of the mattress.

He turned back to face the old man but was at a loss for words.

His embarrassment was only momentary, because the door of the barracks opened and he and the old looked across to see a *Kapo* enter. As the *Kapo* walked under one of the light bulbs, Nixon got a good look at his face. A chill ran down his spine and beads of sweat instantly appeared on his hands and forehead. It was the *Kapo* he had seen yesterday, and now Nixon knew who it was. The *Kapo* approached his bunk, smiled and handed him a book. Without thinking, Nixon reached out to accept it. By the time he had second thoughts and tried to withdraw his arm, it drew back with the book clasped in his hand. Alger Hiss turned on his heels and strode out of the barracks. Nixon stood motionless and watched him depart. After the door banged shut, he looked down at the book. It was a cloth edition of William Shawcross, *Sideshow: Kissinger, Nixon and the Destruction of Cambodia.* Its dog-eared, red dust jacket had a picture of a B-52 disgorging packets of cluster bombs.

*

For readers too young to remember 'Red baiting', Alger Hiss was an American State Department official accused in 1948 of having spied for the Soviet Union in the 1930s. Statutes of limitations had expired for espionage, but he was convicted of perjury in connection with this charge in 1950. Richard Nixon attracted national attention by demanding that Hiss be tried for espionage and by smearing political opponents with the charge of being 'Reds.'

SURVIVING TET

Aristotle rightly distinguished fright from fear. He argued that we experience fright when confronted with immediate danger. This could be the unexpected appearance of a fierce, wild animal or an enemy on the battlefield. We know today that such experiences are accompanied by the release of adrenaline into the bloodstream and fight-or-flight responses. Fear is aroused by thoughts of something terrible that might happen to us. The imagined event is in the future, not in the present, and generally does not release adrenaline. Fright is a short-lived response to immediate threat. It gives us little time for thinking; indeed, our hormones prompt a quicker response by bypassing cognitive processing. Fear is the opposite. We have time, often considerable time, to mull over our situation and what we might do to minimize or escape the dangers we imagine. Fright passes quickly. Fear can linger, and for some, can be a lifelong affliction.

Saigon aroused more fear than fright. At the outset, however, the principal emotion was annoyance and was associated not only with our arrival in that city but with events that made our trip possible. In the late 1960s, I was an assistant professor of political science at The City College of New York (CCNY). My salary was $12,000 a year, just above what a token seller on the subway earned and the income where one qualified for food stamps. I had no money for travel. The United States Information Agency (USIA) came to the rescue. They sent me to Jamaica to give a talk at a local university, making it possible for Carol and me to have holiday there. They paid for travel, room and board, and even an honorarium on the days I lectured. They had recently sent both of us to Iceland over the Thanksgiving break, but that is another story. We wanted to go to New Zealand, Carol's home country, and then to Australia to visit her sister and her family. I called my contact at USIA and he promised to see what he could do. A couple of weeks later he called back with good news: his colleagues in both countries would welcome us and arrange talks and USIA would pay my air fare. He wanted to know if Carol and I would be willing to go to South Vietnam as well. They desperately wanted speakers. We opposed the war but thought it would be interesting to check it out first-hand, so accepted his offer.

Another week passed and USIA called back. On the line was the boss of the official who had offered to host our trip. The Agency had checked up on us, he explained, only to discover that I had given teach-ins against the war and Carol did draft counseling. The Agency did not want to send people to Vietnam who would embarrass the government. I reminded him that the primary purpose of USIA was to inform people about American life and politics, and what better way to demonstrate what democracy was about than by sending a critic of the government to speak? He was not convinced and tried, unsuccessfully, to convince me that my talks would not be well-received. We had committed ourselves to going and they could not now withdraw their offer on political grounds. He promised to call me back.

I told my friend Harrison Salisbury at *The New York Times* about what had transpired. He suggested that I record my next conversation with USIA. We went over what I would say and how I might trap the official to whom I spoke into admitting that protecting the Nixon administration and its policies was so important that USIA was willing to violate its charter and vet speakers on the basis of their politics. I reiterated to this official the value of sending an opponent of the war to speak in Vietnam, and one, moreover, who would in every other respect be an ideal representative for the Agency. He told me the trip was off; USIA would not sponsor me. I told him that I had recorded our entire conversation and that an edited version would be appearing in the new Op Ed section of *The New York Times*. He was stunned, and then speechless when I played the recording back to him. He told me to do nothing precipitous. He would speak to his superiors. To my surprise, a day or two later I received a call from the deputy director of the Agency. They would send me to New Zealand, Australia, Vietnam, and Hong Kong and I in turn would agree not to publish anything about my telephone conversations.

The talks in New Zealand and Australia, at universities and on radio stations, went well. Carol and I had a weeklong idyl in Bali, still untouched at the time by any resort hotels. We then went on to Singapore for a few days, where a friend of Carol's worked in the New Zealand High Commission. Then the adventure began. We flew Air Vietnam from Singapore to Saigon. It was supposed to be a non-stop flight, but we made an unscheduled landing at a dirt strip somewhere in the jungles of Cambodia or Thailand. We were kept aboard the plane but through the window I could make out people loading burlap sacks into the cargo hold. I wondered if it was opium. We then flew to Saigon, and here too there was a puzzling event.

Before docking at the passenger terminal we taxied over to the military part of the airfield where the burlap bags were unloaded and put on a truck. The South Vietnamese military (ARVN) was presumably dealing in drugs and using the airline as a means of transport.

We were met at the gate by a low-ranking American official named Jeanne. She insisted she would hasten our passage through immigration. The reverse turned out to be the case. For whatever reason, we were the last foreigners to be allowed into the country. Her driver picked us up, stowed our backpacks, and we made ourselves comfortable in the back seat. We drove silently, and Carol and I directed out attention to the local scenery as we made our way into the city. Jeanne finally turned to us and in an angry voice exclaimed: "It's people like you who are making us lose this war!" An argument ensued but it quickly became evident that Jeanne was not willing to listen to another point of view or any of the reasons why such a large anti-war movement had developed in the US. At last we arrived at our hotel and went with her to the registration desk. She spoke Vietnamese to the desk clerk and handed us keys to two rooms. I told her we only needed one. She insisted that because we were not married, we would have separate rooms. "We need to be respectful of local customs," she insisted. We waited for her to leave, explained to the hotel desk clerk in French, that one room would suffice. He was happy to accommodate us.

We wondered if Jeanne was representative of the officials we would meet. Fortunately, she was not. The public affairs and the cultural officers – the first and second in command – at the USIS post – USIA overseas was known as USIS -- in Saigon turned out to be against the war. Both explained that they were delighted to sponsor us in part for this reason. We could say what they could not, and they hoped we would say it often and to large audiences. We found widespread disenchantment with the war among US officials and also in the armed forces. The general consensus was that we were fighting to uphold a corrupt regime and exploitative elite, and bound to lose in the longer-term. Of course, we encountered people – more in the military than in civilian agencies – who backed the war, but few of them expected victory.

Physical danger seemed relatively remote in Saigon, although we did hear stories of Americans being killed. Lots of precautions were in place. A friend in the embassy took us to an excellent French restaurant in the downtown area. We approached an utterly nondescript and somewhat rundown commercial building and our host went up and rapped on the metal door. A slat was pulled back, the person inside could see that we were Caucasian, and the door opened. The guard with an automatic weapon welcomed us as he stepped aside. So this was what a speakeasy was like, I thought. However, it was not some crowded, smoky bar but a large dining room, very French in is furniture, décor, menu, and language of service. We had a very good meal and were impressed by the size of the wine list. It was surreal to go from war-time Saigon to somewhere in provincial France, only to then re-emerge in the city again.

Each excursion outside of Saigon was risky and involved fright, not just fear. We flew south to the Mekong Delta on Air America, an airline owned and run by the Central Intelligence Agency. En route south to Cân Tho, our plane was riddled by ground fire and machine gun bullets passed through the wing and the fuselage on either side of our seats. Even though this happened very quickly, I could see the bullet holes marching toward me and breathed a sigh of relief when they missed us. Flying north to Danang was uneventful, but our stay there at "The Alamo" was another story.

The Marines had named the old colonial hotel by the Danang landing strip the Alamo because of its vague resemblance – quite a stretch in my view -- to the eponymous Texan fort. The more appropriate comparison was siege. The Viet Cong fired rockets at us on a regular basis from their well-entrenched position in the hills to the east. One landed close enough to make the spartan but heavy wooden furniture in our room bounce. Sitting on the desk was a spent artillery shell casing recast as a Buddha and etched with acid to give it the patina of age. It was an attractive copy of an old Cambodian statue. I bought it at a shop in Saigon and schlepped it around the country as the concept of swords into Buddhas was so appealing. The shock wave from the shell knocked it off the desk. It fell on its side onto the floor, pushing in one of the spiky protuberances on the Buddha's head. He, of course, retained his pacific expression.

Breakfast the next morning provided comic relief. The Marines shared the air base with the South Vietnamese air force and coming out of their shared mess I encountered a South Vietnamese captain in a uniform with a Road Runner patch on his shirt. A sensible talisman, I thought, to protect him from Wily Coyote. He was whistling one of Papageno's arias from the Magic Flute. That stopped me in my tracks. I asked him in French if he was a Mozart opera lover. "Alors," he replied, "you are familiar with our culture." I laughed, so did he, and I accompanied him to the mess for another cup of coffee. He explained that he was studying voice in Paris but compelled to return home and here he was flying combat missions. I know the opera well and Papageno is something of a coward, shrinking from the challenge of the life-threatening tests that his bold companion Tamino willingly accepts. Presumably, my new friend also recognized the irony.

Later that morning, Carol and I relaxed at the swimming pool inside the low-walled compound. An officer took too much time positioning himself on the high diving board and presented an inviting target to a sniper. There was little left of his head and the rest of him fell off the board, seemingly in slow motion, into the pool. It was closed for the rest of the day. Our host, the public affairs officer, insisting on taking us on an outing, perhaps thinking it would take our mind off the incident. We drove in an armed convey to China Beach, which the Marines used for R & R. It was a long, pristine, sandy beach guarded by entrenched machine gun positions to protect bathers. We had an interesting, but hardly relaxing, afternoon.

A couple of days later we drove north in a Vietnamese army (ARVN) convoy to Hué. Our car was located in the middle of a dozen trucks that proceeded single file along a two-lane road. Two of them were packed with furniture and other belongings of officers. Another truck brought up their girl-friends. A good part of the drive could be described as something of a game between the Viet Cong and ARVN. The Viet Cong had artillery in the mountains that zeroed in as best they could on our road. They periodically fired, hoping to score at hit at those parts of the road that were visible from their position. The drivers knew the danger zones and would reduce their chance of getting hit by breaking up the convoy into component parts and then slowed down or then speeded up when out of sight because of intervening hills. They would emerge into view out of synch with Viet Cong calculations of their time of arrival. Fortunately, the VC gunners had the day off, and when no shells came our way everyone soon relaxed.

We arrived in Hué in the aftermath of the Tet offensive and the US counter-offensive against the occupying Viet Cong forces. Much of the city was destroyed and many of the buildings left standing showed the scars of shrapnel and bullets. The streets had been cleared of debris and were relatively passable. Casualties had been high on both sides. During the brief occupation of the city the Viet Cong eliminated officials and collaborators. In the aftermath of the city's later liberation, the ARVN went on its own killing spree.

We were met by the assistant of the local American cultural affairs officer who drove us to his compound. It was on the outskirts of the city, in a neighborhood of large, private residences. It stood out for its openness. Like all the residences it was set back some distance from the street but not surrounded by stone or cement walls topped with barbed wire and protected by pill boxes and machine gun nests. It had no fence or hedges, just a lawn and a path and driveway leading from the street to the house. There was no sign of damage from the fighting.

Our host offered us tea and we sat on his veranda and became acquainted. Michael – not his real name – was tall, lanky, and somewhere in his fifties. He was soft-spoken, and had a voice that hinted at Mid-Western roots. He had seen our resumés and asked some inquisitive questions about our research and also what brought us to Vietnam. I told him about my encounter with the US Information Agency (USIA) which he thought hilarious.

I had a slew of reciprocal questions for Michael. How did he end up in Hué? How did he survive Tet? And why was his house open and unprotected, unlike any other American compound I had seen in the country? He laughed and said he had a tale to match my own. He explained that he was a homosexual and, while discreet, made no secret about it. Washington found this embarrassing and so posted him to Vietnam – hardly a sought after posting. Saigon found him an embarrassment and sent him to the boonies. Hué was the most distant city to have a cultural affairs officer.

I suggested that it was also the most dangerous. "They did not know that at the time," he assured me. It was just an out-of-the-way place that would make me invisible to all but the most intrepid visitors -- like the two of you."

"Were you here during Tet?" I asked.

"It was quite something" he replied. "The Viet Cong took over the city in a matter of hours and immediately began eliminating the opposition. They had a very liberal view of who their enemies were, killing all officials, South

Vietnamese soldiers, others identified as collaborators, and any Americans they could get their hands on."

"How did you survive?"

"I was very lucky.'

"Surely, it was more than luck. Our compound is entirely open and unprotected. The VC must have known where you were and could have captured you with impunity."

"Maybe I was safe for this reason. Like all Americans with official residences, I receive a hefty monthly allowance for security. Most of my colleagues wall in their compounds and hire guards to protect them. I was never convinced that this did any good. If the VC wanted to get you, they would pick off your guards and scale your walls. From what I've heard, hired guards are likely to run off at the first inkling of a firefight. Like mercenaries everywhere they are in it for the money, and it doesn't pay to get killed."

"So what protected you?"

"I use the funds I receive for security to run a soup kitchen. Twice daily I provide hot meals to anybody in need. Sometimes there is a long line of hungry people, including children, and I feed up to two hundred people a day. You can see for yourself tonight."

"Do you help out?" Carol asked.

"At lunchtime, whenever I am free, and sometimes in the evening. I help serve out on the lawn and talk to the people who come to eat. I've recruited some of them to help and pay them a decent salary. I've also arranged medical care for a few needy people."

"You must be a popular man in these parts?" I suggested.

"I think so, and it might explain why the VC left me in peace. This war is above all a political struggle. The VC is winning because it has successfully framed the conflict as one of national liberation and convinced people that its victory will also bring about a better life for them. I'm doing this in my own small way and the VC would probably lose support by killing me and putting an end to my charity."

"That makes sense."

"Until the US counter-offensive, I had no problem buying supplies and my staff came to work without interference. More evidence, I think, that someone in the National Liberation Front made a decision to leave me alone."

"What happened during the counter-offensive?"

"All hell broke loose. The VC dug in, the US shelled and bombed them, and destroyed much of the city in the process. They routed the VC after twenty-six days, killing thousands of civilians in the process. The generals proclaimed a victory but it was a pyrrhic one. They killed lots of VC but completely alienated the community. It was a political victory for the Viet Cong."

"My soup kitchen is up and running again. The Marines give me food from their larder, and I'm hoping to buy everything I need locally again as I don't want to depend on the military."

"So the Marines haven't killed you either?"

Michael grimaced. "They almost did. One of their shells exploded nearby and Marines in full battle gear approached my compound. I had to march out with a white flag."

"You have protection on both sides," I suggested.

"Seemingly so, and you will meet them tomorrow evening."

"I don't understand."

Michael chuckled. "You'll see."

That evening the three of us had drinks on the veranda and a lovely dinner prepared by Michael's chef. Earlier, Michael spent some thirty minutes on the food line talking to people and reported back to us some of what he had heard. Nobody ever expressed political sentiments. They kept those thoughts to themselves, but he got a sense that people were frightened and fearful of new fighting.

Michael was a well-educated man, having done a degree in Chinese history and literature at Yale. This created another bond between us, as I had done graduate work at Yale. He took the foreign service exam after graduation and joined the State Department, later transferring to the newly created USIA. He had prior postings in Hong Kong and Taiwan. He would use the opportunity to do a master's degree. His specialty was classical Chinese literature, especially the Hundred Schools of the Tang Period. Neither Carol nor I knew anything about the subject, so we quizzed him instead about his life in Hué and his understanding of how his colleagues viewed the war. Most were disillusioned, he thought. Having much local experience in the region, they could not take the domino theory seriously. They regarded the conflict as a largely internal one for which Washington bore considerable responsibility because of its insistence in Geneva in 1954 that the country be temporarily divided in two, and then later encouraging Southern leaders not to hold elections for fear that Ho Chi Minh would emerge the victor. He believed that the US was undermining democracy, not supporting it. Military intervention under President Johnson had only made matters worse. The US could win every firefight but would still lose the war because the regime it supported in the South was now regarded as a corrupt, puppet government.

"Does anybody support the war?" Carol asked.

"Oh yes, some people do, and some of them are quite thoughtful. They fear communism and see it as a worldwide conspiracy. Many also believe that the US will lose face and support throughout the region if it walks away from a commitment it has fought to uphold for so long. But hardly anybody I know supports the militarization of what is, at its core, a political problem. You most often hear these arguments from the military, but there are many officers, even generals – you'll meet one tomorrow night – who question these arguments. They are mostly Marines.

"Why is that?" I asked.

"They are the force mostly closely integrated with the ARVN. They have an accurate sense of what it is worth and how it is likely to melt away if left on its own. They also have their ears closer to the ground than the army and recognize that most villagers value their survival and wellbeing more than anything else. They have no real commitment to either side and will appear to support whoever is the dominant in their vicinity. The minority who are committed almost all support the Viet Cong."

Carol and I were given a tour around the city by Michael's assistant.
Evidence of the fighting was everywhere. The nearby countryside was
pockmarked with shell and bomb craters. It had just rained heavily so they
were filled with water and very visible. The countryside was nevertheless
lush and the local inhabitants went about their business on foot or on the
ubiquitous motor bikes and bicycles. It was a far-cry from the countryside
we had flown over that had been cleared with agent orange and looked like
a lunar surface.

Here, as everywhere else, I had to sing for my supper, but Michael made it
an easy and enjoyable experience. He arranged an informal seminar at his
house as the American library had been destroyed during the fighting. I
met with some half-dozen people, most of them young, and made my talk
about American politics briefer than usual to leave more time to interact
with these participants. I gave my talk in English but the conversation that
followed was a mix of French and English. My interlocutors were intelligent
and well-informed and we had a good discussion about American foreign
policy, the strength and effects of the anti-war movement, and the role of
journalism in the war. They wanted to know how the war and their country
was reported in American media. I explained how coverage had gone from
largely supportive of government policy at the outset but was now largely
opposed, albeit in a restrained manner. Tet was a turning point. It convinced
many journalists that the war was unwinnable, and they passed their views
on to the public,

I asked what kind of outcome they wanted. Nobody volunteered an
answer, but when I pushed them, one of them replied that there were
no good outcomes. A Viet Cong victory would do away with the few
freedoms they had left and not be good for the professional class – to which
they all belonged. A continued American presence meant a high level of
violence and an arbitrarily repressive regime. Others nodded their heads in
agreement. Were they taking a risk attending my seminar? Only a marginal
one, someone replied. It would not put them on any hit list, especially as
our host was a man respected by everyone.

In the early evening, Carol and I helped Michael set up for his dinner party.
He had a chef who would do the food preparation and someone who
came by to serve whenever he entertained. The menu was what today we
would be called fusion. It was Vietnamese with French touches. In addition

to us, Michael was expecting three guests: a Marine general in command of I Corps, responsible for the northern tier of the country; Mr. Trang, a prominent, local businessman; and an elderly Theravada Buddhist priest who lived in a nearby monastery. Michael explained that they met regularly to discuss the mutual love of Chinese literature.

"The general too?" I asked.

"Oh, yes. He is a fluent Chinese speaker and has a good reading command of classical Chinese. So do the other two. But don't worry. They know you are my guests and we will not talk literature tonight."

"There can't be many generals like him in the Corps?"

"Probably not, but don't write off the Marines. Their officers, especially senior ones, are well-educated and often more independently minded than their army and air force counterparts."

The guests arrived at almost the same time. Introductions were made and we were invited to take seats on the veranda. It was a large and comfortable room with a hardwood floor, bamboo furniture, and screened in on three sides. We were offered glasses of rice wine, the traditional ice-breaker in Vietnamese gatherings. The general came across as intelligent, genial, thoughtful, and more interested in drawing out others than in expressing his own views. The Vietnamese businessman, who had arrived in a chauffeur-driven car, was wearing what looked like a very expensive silk suit. He was about forty, agile, fit, and something of an enigma as he said very little. I would have dismissed him as your average successful businessman who liked to flaunt his success had not Michael told me about his interest in and knowledge of classical Chinese literature. His name seemed fitting, as Trang in Vietnamese means "decoration."

The Buddhist priest was a bonze from central casting. He was old and thin, even gaunt, but well preserved and of indeterminate age. He was clean shaven except for some hairs that extended several inches from his chin. He wore a bright orange robe and it moved with him in pleasing, flowing manner. It was big and he was so small that it all but enveloped him. For a man who led a contemplative life he was quite loquacious, although not in English. To accommodate him we spent most of the evening speaking French. Occasionally, Michael would say something in Vietnamese to the businessman, and we had the odd aside in English with the general.

Dinner conversation touched on multiple topics. Carol and I asked the priest questions about his life, his community, and how he had developed an interest in Chinese literature. He had gone to university in Saigon before entering the priesthood and had studied philosophy and literature. Our businessman was also a university graduate. He had wanted to pursue postgraduate studies in Chinese history and literature, but was "persuaded" by his father to enter the family business. The general's experience was not that different. He attended the University of Michigan, funded by the naval reserve program (NROTC) where he did a double major in political science and Chinese history. He went directly into the Marines after graduating and signed up for another four years because they promised to send him to graduate school. He did a PhD in Chinese language and literature at Stanford and then tours of duty in South Korea, South Vietnam, and Quantico, Virginia, before being sent to the Naval War College in Newport, Rhode Island. He did a stint at Marine headquarters and was now back in Vietnam.

Before dinner, I had asked Michael if it was permissible to ask questions about the war and local politics and had received his assurances. I was waiting for the appropriate moment to steer the conversation in this direction but Michael did it for me. We had finished dinner and returned to the veranda, which had cooled off nicely as it was positioned to benefit from the off-shore evening breeze. Our conversation paused as some heavy vehicles, presumably military trucks, passed by the compound.

When the noise subsided, Michael said: "Ned and Carol would like to know how you think all of this will end?"

To my surprise the businessman was the first to speak. "I have little doubt about the outcome. The political pressure on President Nixon to withdraw is enormous but the political right and the generals are telling him to stay the course. As Nixon is a Republican, he has to appease the right more than a Democrat would. I'm guessing that he will withdraw most American forces but step up the bombing."

"I agree," the general said. Nixon is under pressure from opposite directions and a drawdown of troops will take the sting out of the anti-war movement and increased bombing and support for the ARVN will pacify most of the hawks."

"That will leave all of us in the provinces pretty exposed," Michael said.

"I-Corps is already stretched," the general said. "We play a little game with the VC. We occupy a village or two and they withdraw before we arrive. Don't ask where they get their intelligence from. We leave after we think the area is pacified and they immediately move back in. I don't dare bomb the villages because we will kill mostly civilians. The army doesn't want to recognize that their airstrikes, even when successful, are the VC's best recruiting weapon."

"Do you get into frequent firefights with the Viet Cong?" I asked.

"Very rarely these days. The fighting was fierce when we retook the city, and also in the countryside. Within six months it petered out because the VC gave up its military formations and went back to organizing itself as a guerilla force. Small units would occupy villages or conduct ambushes, and most of them against the ARVN."

"Why did you get a bye?"

"I'm not entirely sure. You'd think that killing Americans would build support for a pullout as the antiwar movement benefits from high casualty rates. But we Marines are hard to kill. We're better equipped and better trained than the army for counter-guerrilla warfare. We're vulnerable, of course, but we're going to take out a lot of them for every one of our losses. The Marines are all volunteers, unlike the army, which relies heavily on the draft. So you get more political benefits from killing soldiers, and it costs you less."

"Do you get the same kind of intelligence about them that they do about you?"

"I can't answer that question, of course. But our intelligence is getting better and occasionally we make good use of it. In the last year, however, things have been rather quiet. The VC is directing most of its military effort against the ARVN and more or less leaving us alone."

"Aren't you integrated to some degree with the ARVN?"

"Yes, very much more so than the army. We use these combined units to occupy villages and carry out patrols. The VC on the whole stays clear of them and attacks purely ARVN units. They do so with relative impunity and inflict serious losses. It pays off because it's become increasingly difficult for ARVN to attract recruits or keep officers."

The priest nodded his head. "It's a very effective strategy. Ultimately, the US will have few forces left on the ground. Our friends the Marines may be among the last to go, but go they will. This will leave only the ARVN and it won't hold back the National Liberation Front for long."

"Even if the US continues with its air strikes?" I asked.

"Their tactical air is impressive, but the VC is relatively immune so long as it does not mass its forces."

"But don't you need to do that," I asked, "if you want to take over the South and occupy its cities?"

The priest responded: "If you launch a Tet-like offensive where small, dispersed, and hidden forces suddenly come together all over the country, you overwhelm the American air force and artillery with possible targets. If most VC concentrations are in or near cities, they will be more hesitant to bomb and shell."

"It didn't seem that way during Tet," I suggested.

"Yes and no," the general said. "We bombed and shelled to soften them up before we launched counter-offensives. Without any offensive ground capability we would be less likely to do this as it would cause immense collateral damage for little military advantage."

"And don't forget the North Vietnamese Army," the businessman said. "They too know the likely cost of showing themselves in large units. But they have developed effective ways of moving large numbers of men and equipment through the jungles and mountains where they are all but invisible. I can imagine that many of their units would be in place and come to the support of the Viet Cong. They might even invade directly from the north."

"So you all think the outcome foreordained?" I asked.

"We do," said the businessman. It's only a matter of time. More pressure on the ARVN, an American withdrawal, and then a quick takeover with the help of the North Vietnamese army."

"And you agree?" I looked at the general.

"I do. The ARVN will not put up a real fight against either the VC or an invading Northern army. I wouldn't be surprised if Saigon fell so quickly that not all the Americans could get out."

"What would happen then?"

"Oh, they would be allowed to depart in peace but it would be great propaganda victory for the communists and a humiliation for the US."

"And the longer-term consequences?"

"Not what Washington fears." The general said. There are no dominos to fall. Vietnam will be reunited and Hanoi will solidify its influence in Laos and Cambodia. But further expansion? Hardly likely. There's no love between the Vietnamese and the Chinese but they are dependent on them as long as they are fighting us. The Chinese like it this way and tensions between the countries are likely to increase the more independent the Vietnamese become. The new fault line in Southeast Asia will be the Vietnamese-Chinese border and nationalism will be at the heart of the conflict."

Neither the businessman nor priest offered any dissent. The priest expressed concern for the Chinese community within Vietnam. "These are hardworking people who contribute to the economy. Deteriorating relations with China, which is likely, will create domestic tensions and could lead to the kind of violence we see elsewhere in the region against local Chinese immigrant communities."

"Is there nothing that can be done politically to prevent the violent outcome you all foresee?" Carol asked.

"Very unlikely," said the businessman. "The US and its puppet regime will never agree to free elections, which is the only political way to resolve the problem."

"I concur," said the general. "Nixon can't hand over the South to the Viet Cong, which would quickly lead to unification. He would arouse fierce opposition in the Pentagon and in his own party. The Democrats would probably also join the feeding frenzy. Elections would provide the cover he needs as the National Liberation Front would certainly win. So long as

Nixon and Kissinger refuse to recognize the struggle in Vietnam is a local one with largely local implications, not a communist challenge to American credibility, they will never give in."

"That's the problem," Michael agreed. "They are prisoners of their ideology and as a result acting against the real interests of their country."

"The end will still come," the businessman insisted. "We all agree on the scenario."

"What a tragedy!" the general exclaimed. "We know what will happen but have to let events take their course. If only the administration could agree to some face-saving agreement – I'm certain that Hanoi would push the VC to agree to it and postpone their takeover of the South for a couple of years. But it won't happen, at least as long as Nixon and Kissinger run American foreign policy."

"So the fighting will go on and more people will die," said the priest.

"A lot more," said the businessman.

"Too bad," Carol said, "that the warring parties won't delegate authority to the three of you."

The priest agreed. "We would have it straightened out in no time."

"It's time to go," said the businessman. Everyone rose and thanked Michael for a pleasant evening and delicious dinner. The businessman offered to drive the priest back to his compound. The general also had a driver who had returned to pick him up. We said our farewells by the door and Michael's local guests went on their way.

We started to cleanup but Michael stopped us, saying his staff would deal with the mess in the morning. "Come join me for a nightcap," he insisted.

We had all been abstemious so I readily agreed. Michael came back from the kitchen with a bottle of Napoleon cognac and three glasses. We went back out to the veranda, where the breeze had picked up. We sat down and Carol reached out for one of the glasses as cognac was her favorite tipple.

"Just whom do you think those three men are?" Michael asked.

"What do you mean?" I asked.

Michael looked me in the eye. "The general is exactly whom he claims to be. I think he's an excellent officer as the level of violence has gone down considerably since he assumed command."

"Would the Pentagon be impressed by that metric?" I asked.

"Perhaps not, but let's come back to this question."

"The businessman is the regional political representative of the National Liberation Front."

"You're kidding?" Carol said.

"No," Michael replied. He has a direct line to the Viet Cong."

"How do you know that?" I asked. "It's no big secret. He never acknowledges his position but he is the go-to person for journalists, and even government officials who want to know what the Viet Cong think about something."

"The general must know this then", Carol said.

"Of course. It's one of the reasons the three men meet regularly."

"And what about the priest?" I asked.

"He's a spokesman for Hanoi. The regime has been very careful to treat Buddhists well and many have become prominent in the nationalist movement. I suppose they are not all that opposed to communism as they live an ordered life and take the equivalent of vows of poverty."

"And this is well known too?" I asked.

"Not at all. I would guess he has confided his position to only a few people."

"And you are obviously one of them."

"Yes, I am."

"Why are you telling us?" I asked.

"I don't think it can do any harm, even if his secret became public. You are really interested in the conflict and free of the usual American prejudices. You are also leaving tomorrow for Saigon, and then, if I remember correctly, for Hong Kong. You're not a local player but someone who might talk some political sense into people back home."

"I assume the general also knows?"

"Indeed. We meet on a regular basis, as I told you, to talk about Chinese literature. After an hour or so I disappear and leave the three men on the veranda. I like to take evening walks.

"Is that safe?"

"For me it is. They talk among themselves and presumably exchange intelligence that each wants the other to know about."

"How remarkable!" Carol exclaimed.

"Sometimes I suspect," Michael said, "they make arrangements among themselves. Perhaps it's not accidental that the rate of violence and casualties on all sides is lower here than elsewhere in the country."

"It wouldn't be the first time something like this happened," I said. "Toward the end of the War, a few German commanders in northern Italy made arrangements with the resistance to avoid further bloodshed. The deals were brokered by priests – and that may be the case here. Both sides went through the motions of hunting each other down but it was more a charade than a reality."

"Interesting," Michael said. "Our general reads everything he can get his hands on about World War II."

Postscript

In 2008 I was a professor at Dartmouth College. Carol and I occasionally went on cruises sponsored by the alumni association where one of us would give three lectures and socialize with the Dartmouth grads. The highpoint was a week in the Antarctic. A year or two later I was offered the opportunity, solo on this occasion, to lecture on a month-long, private jet, tour of Asia with the pretentious title: "The Lands of the Great Buddha." The first destination was Lhasa, Tibet, the final one, Osaka, Japan, and in between we touched down in various locales in China, Outer Mongolia, India, Nepal, Cambodia, and Vietnam.

I made one of my lectures on the war in Indochina and was very keen to see how Vietnam had changed in the almost forty years since I had been there. Our first destination was Danang and even on the approach to the airport the difference was notable. When we landed during the war we did a steep angle descent, literally falling out of the sky and hitting the runway with a resounding bang. It was not good for the plane, and a little unnerving for the passengers, but it presented a far more difficult target to the enemy. This time we came in on a long glide path and made a smooth touchdown. But I could still tell it was Danang because waterlogged shell craters on either side of the runway were still visible.

We taxied over to a relatively new terminal, disembarked, and entered the customs hall. To our surprise we were greeted by a bevy of school children who presented us with flower leis and performed a dance for us. They were extraordinary. No more than five and six years of age, they executed an elaborate five minute dance routine with surprising skill and coordination. Their teacher must have put them through hours of practice to achieve this level of proficiency. The faces revealed joy and the little girl who gave me the lei also gave me a big hug. Other than the few immigration officials and one policeman, also enjoying the show, there were no other uniforms in sight and nobody carried a weapon.

Danang had been rebuilt, people looked healthy and well-fed, motorbikes were still ubiquitous, and capitalism was on the march. Shops of all kinds advertised their wares, many of them selling imported goods, and most of them from China. We spent a couple of hours in the city, including an hour in a museum featuring local archeological finds and art from different eras of Vietnamese history. There were many Buddhas and they ran the gamut from crass to delicate.

To my surprise and delight our hotel was in China Beach. There were no check points or machine gun nests on the road there and we arrived to find a strip of modern looking hotels along the strand. We checked into one of the newest, and the trip's doctor and I decided to go exploring. We walked along the sandy beach, met some local kids, and joined a pick-up football game. A quick reconnaissance of other hotels and cafes revealed that most of the clientele was Vietnamese. There were lots of families, mostly middle class, and day trippers from Danang and surrounding areas. The vibes were excellent, the locals willing to chat with foreigners, and more hotels under construction. The goal, the hotel's bartender told us, was to become a kind of Miami Beach and attract foreigners as well as locals.

The following morning, we made a day trip to Hué, where the memory of the past and the scenes of the present were just as surreal. I gave a lecture on the bus ride up and told the story that I have written here. We visited the Thien Mu pagoda, the old imperial city, and the tomb of the Emperor. I had no time to search for Michael's house but wondered what had become of him, the general, the businessman, and the priest. Were any of them still alive? What did they think of today's Vietnam? What would Lyndon Johnson, Richard Nixon and their hawkish advisors think? For better or worse, Vietnam was a bulwark against China, had not encouraged uprisings elsewhere in Southeast Asia, was increasingly capitalist, and beginning to open up a bit politically. In retrospect, the war seemed even more senseless.

FOO FIGHTERS

Sgt. First Class Tony Mazzarini walked across the unlit runway to "Beanie," a B-17 G that sat the grass at Horham Field in Sussex, England. The base was home to the 95th Bombardment Group of the US Army Air Force. By the end of the war in Europe it would claim 425 German aircraft shot down, more than any other Eighth Air Force Bomb Group. It was the first group to attack Berlin, and that was tonight's mission again.

Sgt. Mazzarini took a look at the setting sun and then into the open nose of the plane. He reached for the wooden strip just inside to ease the pressure on his hands as he pulled himself up. Those lacking gymnastic skills entered through the back door. As tail gunner, Tony should have used this entrance, but he prided himself on his ability to climb in through the nose. It had become something of a talisman to him, and he was taking no chances on this, his 30th and final mission. The air force used to require 25 missions, now it demanded 30, and scuttlebutt had it would soon be upped to 35.

Their B-17 carried ten crewmembers. Four were gunners with assigned positions. The other six had primary missions of pilot, co-pilot, navigator, bombardier, engineer, and radio operator. They also served as flexible gunners. The tail gunner was the most important gunner on the B-17. He protected the rear of the aircraft with twin .50 cal. machine guns. German pilots gained a healthy regard for the tail guns. They changed their tactics and adopted the "12 o'clock" attack, coming in straight on toward the front of the plane with a closing speed of over 500 mph.

Tail gunners were in a dangerous position. They stayed in the center of the fuselage for takeoffs and landings. Once aloft, they crawled back to their motorized, ball-shaped turret and its bicycle type seat, where they assumed a kneeling position for the duration of the mission. Like other crewmembers they wore leather jackets lined with fleece, helmets, gloves, and insulated boots. The tail was drafty, and gunners had to fight off frostbite and continually clear frost from their turret windows because without a clear line of sight they and their aircraft were sitting ducks. In addition to spotting and firing at German fighters, tail gunners relayed information to bombardiers and navigators about the effects of bombing, other bombers that had been hit, shot down, or unable to keep up with the formation.

Sgt. Mazzarini stood near the bomb bay behind the radio operator. He listened to the engines start one at a time and increase in noise and pitch as the pilot put them through their paces. The noise dropped as he throttled back and waited for the signal to move on to an active runway. Runway was something of a misnomer, but a reassuring term; there was no pavement, only grass and dirt with markers to delineate the pathways for planes.

The engines revved up and the bomber lurched forward to take its place in the downwind queue. For the next five minutes, Tony knew, it would be stop and start as planes turned on to face the wind and took off with those still on the ground moving forward into the next position. This procedure was repeated on three parallel taxi and takeoff runways, so three bombers would roar into the air at roughly the same time. This made it easier for them to assume their box formation before approaching enemy territory.

Finally, it was their turn. Tony could see nothing as he was not near a window, but he could feel the bomber turning to the right and presumably aligning itself for takeoff. Not a moment too soon, he grabbed a handrail as the pilot opened the four throttles and with a jerk the bomber lurched forward. It gradually gained speed, with the wheels bumping along the ground and the fuselage shaking until they rose into the air and began to gain altitude.

Sgt. Mazzarini thought about the bombers that were aloft or preparing to take off. If past experience was a guide, there would be several dozen from Horham and they would join up with hundreds of others stationed in numerous air bases along the east coast of England. This armada would have fighter protection – P-47 Thunderbolts and P-51 Mustangs -- both equipped with expendable wing tanks. This gave them the range to escort the bombers to and from Berlin. With their "little friends" to protect them bomber survival rates had improved. It provided the justification for General Henry "Hap" Arnold to up the required mission number.

Thirty minutes into the flight Sgt. Mazzarini was feeling stiff and desperately in need of scratching an itch on his right thigh. There was nothing he could do about it, as he was stuck in his seat in the back turret for the duration of the mission. He could not undo his coveralls or pull down the full-length

BVDs underneath. He tried to concentrate on something else, focusing for a while on a star in the cloudless sky. He had urinated twice before suiting up and hoped his bladder would stay quiescent for the duration of the flight. Not everybody's did, but the rest of the crew had some mobility and with it the possibility of relieving themselves.

Combat, even its anticipation, had unexpected and uncontrollable effects on crewmembers. On his first mission Sgt. Mazzarini had crapped in his pants, but only after fighting off three Messerschmitts and possibly downing one of them. It was the flak that got to him. It was nearly random and there was nothing planes could do to avoid it other than to break formation. And that was unthinkable. The flak was coming up heavy as they approached Brunswick and watched two planes get hit. One burst into flames and slewed to the right before heading straight toward the earth. The other bomber lost part of a wing, and he was surprised and relieved to see chutes opening beneath it. Then his plane rocked, hit by the shock wave of an exploding anti-aircraft shell. It happened again, and he heard a couple of zings as pieces of flak penetrated the fuselage. That's when he lost it. The flak and shaking diminished and then disappeared after their bombs were released. He could feel the plane lift and bank to the starboard. There were no fighters to contend with on the long journey home, as they preferred to pick off stragglers.

That was twenty-five missions back. Sgt. Mazzarini was a different man now, for better and worse. He was still terrified every time he flew, but cool in combat and part of a team. He had come to terms with death in a way he would never have thought possible. It made him a better machine gunner. He had four definite and two probable kills. On his first mission he shot at Jerry because he was coming after him. After a few missions and the loss of friends to fighters or flak, it became personal. He wanted to kill the bastards. By ten missions he got over that. It was no longer personal. He came to believe that the Germans didn't want to fly their Messerschmitts and Focke-Wulfs anymore than his crews did their B-17s. Nobody had any choice in the matter. It was kill-or-be-killed, and he wanted to get home, and all the more so as his mission number crept upwards towards twenty-five. He now killed with impunity, but with regrets. He wondered how he was going to readjust to civilian life driving a delivery truck in and around Natick, Massachusetts.

Sgt. Mazzarini also thought about what they were risking death for. Bombing cities was targeting women, children, and old men. Maybe, if they were lucky, and their ordnance landed on target they would destroy some factories and kill some workers. But he knew from briefings and discussions with his bombardier that war plants were better protected and bombing missions now focused more on city-busting. He could almost sympathize with German pilots who were trying to protect the civilians below. He would do the same thing in the circumstances. He certainly hoped that the bombing would, as claimed, hasten the end of the War. There was no point to it otherwise. His reverie ended abruptly when two fighters came into view at 2 o'clock and perhaps a thousand feet above them. He breathed a sigh of relief when he identified them as P-47 Thunderbolts. They were two "little friends" signaling the bomber squares that their escorts were here. Little friend, he thought, although a term of endearment among bomber crews, was quite a misnomer as the P-47, armed with eight .50-caliber machine guns, was the heaviest fighter ever built. The P-47s shot by, but at a safe distance in case some novice gunner mistook them for Germans.

Their flight was uneventful until they were almost over their target. He could see searchlights below attempting to fix on their bombers and provide targets for the anti-aircraft gunners. There were bursts of flak from the exploding shells they fired, but none were close. He felt the usual anxiety and then sense of relief when the plane rose into the air after disgorging its bombs. It banked to the starboard and headed home in the midst of a large and still intact formation.

Then something unusual happened. He noticed lights, some half-dozen in a line, moving quickly towards them at 9 o'clock high. He moved his guns into position wondering what they were. Jerry never flew in a line and knew better than to come at them from almost any position other than head or out of the sun. He waited, fingers poised above his triggers, for his adversary to attack, but they never did. The lights passed behind and above him at what he estimated to be some fantastic speed. They were gone and did not return. The remainder of the flight home was uneventful. He saw nothing beneath him as Europe and England were blacked out. The first indication that they were close to base was the sound of engines being throttled back and the sense that they were losing altitude. He crawled out of his turret and into the center of the plane. He felt the wheels touch the ground, the bomber jump into the air before touching ground again, and slowing down and taxiing to their usual parking place.

There was a race to get out of and away from the bomber. It was the last time they would fly in *The Beanie* and they wanted to put distance between it and themselves. The one exception was the radio operator. He kissed his hand and held it against the fuselage. The pilot shook hands and hugged everyone before they boarded the waiting Jeep. A photographer in uniform took some candid snaps and later asked permission to send them to *Yank* magazine. The debriefing went quickly and the colonel in charge and just about everyone else offered congratulations to him and his crew. Within the week they would be heading Stateside.

Sgt. Mazzarini had time on his hands, much of which he spent reading. The base had a surprisingly good library that included lots of crime fiction. He had liberty to go into town and twice borrowed a bicycle to do so. He liked the exercise, and even more, getting away from the base. He had heard that the English were hostile to Americans, whom they described as "overpaid, oversexed, and over here." He had encountered a warm welcome in the tiny village of Horham and its Blue Dragon pub. He preferred it to the Red Feather, which the Army had established as a club for non-commissioned officers. In the Blue Dragon, he could drink English beer, which to his surprise he quite liked, and chat with locals. They were as pleased as he was to talk to someone from far off who spoke the same language and was fighting the same fight.

Sgt. Mazzarini made sure he was on hand when the bombers from subsequent missions returned. The Americans flew mostly daylight missions, and the British at night. The bombers could return anytime from late afternoon to early evening. It was the tensest moment on the base. Fire engines, ambulances, and medics were readied, and flares were sent aloft, if necessary, to guide the bombers home. Everyone counted aircraft, hoping they would all return safely, but they almost never did. One aircraft missing was depressing, and several gone created an almost intolerable tension. People would patiently wait for stragglers, hoping they would make it back to base. Some did, not infrequently flying on one or two of their four engines.

A couple of weeks back there was total silence when a lone bomber approached, almost an hour late, powered by only one engine – experienced airmen had no difficulty in determining this on the basis of the sound it made. The last engine sputtered and then went silent and then the plane appeared but on a dangerously low glide path. It touched down and ploughed through some hedges before coming to a stop. Fire engines, ambulances and medics rushed to it. The crew was unscathed even though their bomber was badly shot up. On other occasions stragglers landed at other airfields, or, if they were unlucky, ditched in the Channel. Unlike German pilots during the Battle of Britain, who called it "die Scheise Kanal" [the Shit Canal] because there was little hope for them if they went down, allied crews welcomed its sight. It meant they were close to home, and if they had to ditch, the British navy had a string of ships beneath them whose job it was to rescue airmen.

There would be sorrow on the base when returning crews recounted tales of lost bombers, especially those from which no chutes were seen to have opened. There would be joy when word arrived by telephone that a crew had landed somewhere else or had been picked up at sea. The most extraordinary tale was the unexpected return – a full month after being reported missing -- of five crew of "Ditchard's Bice," a bomber that went down in France. Local farmers hid the men until the Resistance could escort them in several night journeys to the coast. They were rowed out to a French fishing boat that delivered them to a British corvette. Their only regret, which got a good laugh, was giving up French wine for British tea.

Sgt. Mazzarini made no sense of the lights he had seen over Berlin on his last mission and asked around to see who else might have witnessed them. There had been talk of secret German weapons but these lights never threatened the bombers. Crews from a number of bombers had seen the lights and were equally baffled. Sgt. Mazzarini discovered that two subsequent missions had encountered them. On both occasions, American fighters set out after the mysterious lights, but to no effect. His informants said that the lights had made what appeared to be right angle turns and then accelerated at unheard of speeds. The fighter pilots gave them the nickname of "foo fighters," because the moment you went after them they high-tailed it.

Word got around that Sgt. Mazzarini was asking questions about the strange lights. One of the P-51 pilots sought him out to exchange information. The pilot confirmed what the sergeant had heard and offered his opinion that the lights were some kind of alien craft. Nothing man-made could possibly accelerate so fast and no human being could withstand the strain of a right angle turn at high speed. "But please don't tell anyone I said this," he insisted.

The day before Sgt. Mazzarini and his crew were scheduled to depart, they were summoned along with other crews to a special briefing. Nobody had any idea of what it was about and there was considerable speculation. The sergeant's crewmates worried that it was some large and dangerous mission that they would have to fly before returning to the States.

When everyone was seated, the colonel who briefed them regularly entered the room. They stood to attention and were told to be at ease.

"This is not a mission briefing," he announced.

The flyers immediately assumed more relaxed postures.

"I know that several missions encountered strange lights over Germany but were never attacked by them. Fighter pilots gave chase and the lights disappeared at unbelievable velocities. The good news is that there is no evidence they are German weapons. Frankly, we do not know what they are. Some of the scientists think they are weather phenomena. Headquarters Eighth Air Force is investigating and has sent a team over to interview any of you who have seen the lights. They recently completed their interviews of fighter pilots.

"How typical," a voice in the back said. "Once again fighter pilots come first."

There were chuckles in the audience.

The colonel pointed to a sergeant seated at a desk close to one of the doors. "On your way out make an appointment with him to be debriefed if you've seen these lights, or anything else strange for that matter. These interviews won't take long, I promise you. One more thing, HQ is adamant that no word of this must get out to the public or even to allied officers. We will, of course, confer with the British, but only at the highest levels."

A hand rose in the audience,

"Captain, you have a question?"

"I do sir."

"Go ahead."

"If we encounter these objects again, what should we do?"

The colonel turned to a major in the front row. "Captain O'Brien will answer your question. He's head of the interview team."

The captain stood and faced the bomber crews. "They're lights, not objects. Observe them carefully without changing course and report what you see at the post-mission debriefing. We all know how hard it is to estimate the speed and course of other aircraft. Several fighter pilots reported these lights traveling at velocities of thousands of miles an hour and making perpendicular turns. Nothing known to man can turn on a dime like that and any being inside would be crushed by gravity. That's one reason why our experts think we are dealing with some kind of natural phenomenon. But keep your eyes open and report back."

The colonel paused and looked around the room. "Any more questions?"

No hands appeared.

"Then you are dismissed."

Sgt. Mazzarini got on the queue to sign up for a debriefing, which he had later that afternoon. The captain with whom he spoke asked him how many missions he had flown and other background information that was all in his service record. How typical of the army, he thought. When finally asked about the lights he reported matter-of-factly that they were orange in color, followed his plane, and then zoomed away at fantastic speed.

"How close do you think they were?"

"I have no idea. They had no observable shape, they were just lights. Like Christmas lights, but moving. At first slowly, at least relative to me, then much, much faster."

The captain asked him a few more questions and then sent him on his way.

Foo fighters did not impinge on Sgt. Mazzarini's consciousness for the remainder of his short stay in England. He packed up his kit, said good-bye to his friends on the base and in town, and had a rough but uneventful ride home on a Liberty ship that had been converted to a troopship. He read when the seas permitted, played low stakes poker, and gossiped with new acquaintances.

On December 13, 1945, Supreme Headquarters Allies Expeditionary Force in Paris issued a press release about the lights observed by bomber and fighter pilots. Newspapers in Britain and the US picked up the story. *The New York Times* speculated that it was some kind of new German weapon. In January 1945, *Time* devoted a story to the sightings, reporting that pilots were followed by high speed "balls of fire." According to the magazine, scientists dismissed the sightings as illusions caused by flak bursts or St. Elmo's Fire.

Once home, Sgt. Mazzarini tried to put the war behind him. He had not talked about his combat experiences to anyone and felt most relaxed with other veterans. They met at a local tavern where they would drink moderately and talk about where they were stationed and what they did in general terms. They offered support and advice to members of their circle who were having a hard time readjusting to civilian life.

Sgt. Mazzarini's family quickly learned not to ask questions about the missions he had flown. He was willing to talk about the friends he had made in the service from all over the country, how much he liked and admired the English, and the close relationship he established with other members of his bomber crew. At his first Sunday family dinner his twelve-year old nephew Joey asked him if he had seen the article in *Time* about Foo-Fighters.

"I haven't. What did it say?

Joey summarized the article.

"The reporters are wrong. They're neither German nor illusions. I've seen them myself."

"You have?" Tony asked.

Conversation stopped among the eight family members.

"I have, and I'm not alone. Over Berlin they approached from the rear and as tail gunner I had them in my sights. I thought at first they were Jerries, but they were lights that had no substance as far as I could tell.

They didn't attack and whizzed by at phenomenal speed. They were seen by other bombers and by crews on other missions. P-51s took off after them on more than one occasion. They're the fastest fighter we have, and they never got close. The fighter jocks said the lights ran rings around them and then disappeared.

"Are you sure they're not German?" Joey asked. "The papers have stories of secret Kraut weapons. One of my school friends says maybe they developed some kind of anti-gravity plane like in the comics."

"For a start, Joey,.. they're Germans, not Krauts. And the lights never attacked. They make right angle turns in which gravity would crush any human pilot."

"What if they are remote controlled?" he asked.

"That's certainly possible. But they would still need a propulsion system beyond anything we have imagined."

"Could they be aliens? Is the government covering it up?"

"That's a bit far-fetched."

Sgt. Mazzarini's father broke in at this point. "Joey, I think your questioning has gone far enough. Tony wants to put his wartime experiences behind him."

"It's OK, Dad," Tony said. "Joey's interested in what goes on around him. I was the same at his age, and I still am, I think."

Tony looked across at Joey, who was helping himself to another forkful of homemade ravioli. "I really don't know what they are. I can tell you that the Army brass were really interested and interviewed anyone who had seen the lights. We were all told not to talk about it to anyone. But now it's in the newspapers, and *Time* magazine, you say?"

"That's right," said Joey.

"So much for secrets. There's one thing I do know, Joey. Conspiracy theories are bunk. Take the nonsense some Republicans are peddling about Roosevelt knowing beforehand about the Japanese attack on Pearl Harbour. If this were true, lots of people in the government would have been in on it and someone one would have leaked it to the press."

"Why would they do that?" Joey asked.

"Joey!" his mom said. "My brother has hardly touched his ravioli. Let him eat."

Tony smiled at his sister. He had indeed just taken his first bite, which he carefully chewed and swallowed and then lowered his fork to spear another.

"Mom, you're the best. You sure don't eat like this in the army."

"I made this *primo* with you in mind. I know it's your favorite.

"But leave some room for the cotoletta."

"Veal? Is there any to be had?"

"Only on the *mercato nero*, and I would never buy there. It's pork. I've been saving red points for some time for a welcome home dinner."

"Why would they leak the story?" Joey asked a second time.

"For many reasons," his uncle Tony replied. "The newspaper offers them money. They want to embarrass some official or the bureaucracy. They seek publicity or want to demonstrate their importance."

"Even high-raking officers and government officials?"

"Especially high-ranking officers and officials."

"Don't turn your nephew into a cynic, Tony," his father said.

"It's OK, Dad. It's time he learned something about the world he'll never be taught in school."

Tony put his fork down and looked across the table to Joey. "Governments and armies are sloppy. They are wasteful, often ineffective, and always leak like sieves. They don't build loyalty, only alienation."

Tony reached for another piece of ravioli with his fork. "Do you know what alienation is?"

"I think so. It's a kind of disenchantment."

"Exactly. Large organizations encourage people to think of themselves first. To the extent there is any camaraderie and loyalty it is among the alienated. All the aircrews despised the Eighth Air Force. The people who run it treated us as expendable and replaceable. Our loyalty was to one another."

"What about loyalty to our country and winning the war?"

"For the most part we bombed German cities and killed civilians. I have no idea if it shortened the war. As for Jerry, I hated him at the beginning but came to believe that he was also just doing his job. I shot at him when he got close, but got no pleasure from it."

"Did you kill lots of Germans?"

"Let's stay on the subject of leaks. The point I'm trying to make is that it is all but impossible for armies and governments to keep secrets. It rules out successful conspiracies. They generally require action – or, I guess, non-action, in the case of FDR and Pearl Harbor. Either way, a number of people have to be in in the know, and there's just no way all of them will take their secret to the grave."

"So you don't think foo fighters are aliens? Joey asked.

"I have no idea what they are. But there's no way the army air force could know they are aliens and keep it mum. They did their best to keep reports of these lights under wraps and the newspapers are already on to them."

"Aliens would really be exciting."

"So would finishing your ravioli," said Joey's mom.

PHYSICIAN, HEAL THYSELF!

Dr. Segal did his best to sympathize with all of his patients and help them as far as he could. This generally meant putting them on the right drugs, monitoring their dosages, observing their behavior, and listening to their self-reporting. Psychotropic drugs had brought about a revolution in psychiatry, but not without cost. Early in his career he had poo-pooed the objections some patients had to taking drugs, many of them young and suffering from depression, who feared that it would change who they were. He had come to appreciate their concerns as he watched people he medicated become different selves. They were better able to cope with life but became more accepting of the world around them and more reconciled to fitting in. He would not like to become such a person.

This morning Dr. Segal had two sessions scheduled in a relatively new ward that he had helped to pioneer. It was for people who were helpless in the outside world because they could not remember their passwords. He and his colleagues called it password recall syndrome and were hoping that the next edition of the Diagnostic Statistical Manual would recognize it as a new clinical disorder. There were a growing number of people, most, but not all of them, elderly, who floundered when they had to recall a string of numbers and letters. With old people this was more understandable because there was much else they could not remember. With the young it was different. They showed no signs of dementia and remembered all kinds of other things. For whatever reason, people of all ages, ethnic backgrounds, and education levels were revealing an increasing difficulty in retaining passwords – even those with only four numbers. He was treating them with traditional and new drugs, hoping one or more would prove promising.

With a smile on his lips he punched in the code to admit him to the ward and sauntered down to the consulting room. Today he was meeting with two patients: an older woman who had a meltdown in a mall, and a younger woman, a new patient, who was responsible for a serious password mishap. He had proscribed a mild dose of tranquilizer for the former and was hoping to proscribe something more experimental for the latter.

The ward was cheery in its appearance. There were wide hallways, high ceilings, light wooden railings and doors, and windows that looked out on to a garden. Patient rooms were on the side with the windows and the consulting rooms and office on the other. There were plants everywhere and the ward looked more like a hotel than a hospital because none of the patients were immobile or seriously ill physically. There was no sign of walkers, IV stands, monitors, or any of the other devices normally on display in hospital wards and corridors.

The cheeriness was deceptive. Everyone understood it was a hospital and many of the patients were more depressed than those in other hospital wards. They knew they would be here longer than people who were recuperating from illnesses or operations and also less capable of facing the world once released. They had accordingly tried to make their rooms and the ward as a whole more like home. There was the occasional picture on the wall and the woman he was to see first had a cat. The animal had caused a major row in the hospital because pets were strictly forbidden. Mrs. Mahoney insisted that it was her support cat and that she would suffer grievously without it. The hospital administration rejected her request but backed down when word got around and other patients rallied to her support. The psychiatrists were furious.

*

Mrs. Mahoney knocked politely on the door to the consulting room. The doctor invited her in and pointed to a comfortable looking leather chair. She sat down, still cradling her cat, a sedate black-and white creature with luminous green eyes. After exchanging the usual pleasantries Dr. Segal got down to business. Mrs. Mahoney was sensitive about any suggestion that she was psychologically unfit, and he tried to bring her around to her problem by circuitous means. She was not the only patient in denial about her condition and, as psychiatrists had long understood, the first and most important step toward a cure was for patients to acknowledge their problem.

Mrs. Mahoney needed considerable encouragement to reach this threshold. His prior efforts had run into a stone wall of defense mechanisms. She denied that she had a problem. It was other people who made unreasonable demands on her. She was making another version of this argument this morning and he was beginning to think that maybe she was paranoid.

"As I've told you before," Mrs. Mahoney said, "there's nothing wrong with me. I'm hardly alone in struggling with passwords. If you hospitalized everyone who couldn't remember them you'd have to build more psychiatric wards than prisons. And while we're on that subject most people behind bars don't belong there either."

"Is that so?"

"It certainly is. More than half of them are imprisoned because they're Black. White society discriminates against them in every way and then punishes them for rebelling."

"Can we return to your problem with passwords?"

"I'm trying to tell you it's not my problem. Everybody I know has difficulty in recalling passwords. You need them for everything from the opening your car door or buying anything with a credit or debit card. You can't use the same password for multiple accounts without putting yourself at risk, and for the same reason, you need to change them every few months. They used to be four digits now they are longer, require a mix of capital and lower case letters, and punctuation marks. Next they will want me to jiggle my phone to the right or left before I key something in.

"All you need to do is change your passwords periodically. Then there would be no problem."

"No problem you say? I would have to remember them. How do you expect me to do that? It's not easy to come up with some jumble with letters, numbers, and symbols that means something to you and will stick in your head. It's impossible to do this for twenty different accounts or devices – and then to do it again and again every few months. I'm a person, not a damn machine."

"But other people do it," Dr. Segal reminded her in a gentle tone of voice.

"Are you sure?" came the quick rejoinder.

"I am. They get on with their lives. Somehow they have figured out how to cope."

"Some have, I do not doubt. I don't know how they do it. But many more are like me. They struggle to remember passwords. And so many of these passwords are totally unnecessary. Last week I had to get one to access the bus schedule. This is public information and there is no reason whatsoever for some silly password."

"You think we could do without them?"

"Yes. For almost everything but banking. And I bank in person. The tellers are nice people and there is good free coffee. Although they tried to close my branch last year , protests from people like me saved it. They want us all to bank online or at their machines."

"Mrs. Mahoney, would you be willing to up your drug regimen? We could reduce your anxiety and make you better able to cope.

Mrs. Mahoney did not reply. Her cat wiggled free, jumped out of her arms on to the floor, made its way to Dr. Segal and began brushing against his right trouser leg. Dr. Segal pulled his leg back, but the cat moved a few inches forward to rub against it again. He tried gently to push her away. She resisted at first, but then drew back and leaped into his lap. He was taken by surprise and jumped up. The cat, thrown off his lap, landed effortlessly on the floor and looked up to face Dr. Segal. He looked down in horror at the beast, who stared back at him for a moment and then sauntered over to her owner's chair and curled up at the base of one of its legs.

Mrs. Mahoney was greatly amused by this episode and its implicit reversal of the power balance between doctor and patient.

"Can you control your cat, please!" Dr. Segal said.

Mrs. Mahoney smiled. "I'm sorry, she seems drawn to you."

"I can't imagine why."

"Neither can I."

"Do you understand why you are here, Mrs. Mahoney?"

"Yes and no, Dr. Segal."

"Would you care to elaborate?"

"I am here because society insists you have multiple passwords that you change on a regular basis. And I cannot do that."

"There's more to the story, isn't there?"

"Well, yes. I threw a hissy fit in a shopping mall when I was denied access to the garage where I had parked my car."

"May I suggest that from what I heard a hissy fit does not quite describe your behavior?"

"It's a matter of opinion, I suppose."

"I would call it a meltdown."

"If you like."

"Do you want to talk about it?

"Not really."

"I think it would be helpful for you to do so."

"If you insist."

"I'm merely suggesting."

"There's not much to say, and I gave you an overview in an earlier session."

"Give me a more elaborate account if you wouldn't mind."

"Well, I went shopping to buy a birthday present for my grandson. He's going to be twelve and is a big sports fan. He also plays the oboe. Did I tell you that?"

'No, you didn't. But it's you I want to hear about."

"He's a fine musician and a good athlete, and, of course, a good student. He doesn't yet know what he wants to be when he grows up but that's natural at his age."

"Mrs. Mahoney, could we return to your meltdown?"

"I bought Liam a keyboard. He's been longing for an upgrade from the one he has had for several years. He really plays it very well."

"Mrs. Mahoney, please."

"I went to pay with a credit card and the bank sent me an SMS with a code to validate the purchase. But I temporarily forgot my new phone code and made the mistake of trying three times to get it right. The phone would not unlock, the purchase would not go through, and trying to use another credit card would not help because they too just send an SMS to my phone. I left the store with a great sense of frustration, went to the café in the mall for a cup of tea to calm down. I swiped my credit card, but it was rejected because of what happened in the store. Fortunately, the other card worked. I drank my tea and headed for the parking garage, where I needed a password to enter. I had reserved a space online and they sent me a code. I got into my phone without a problem at home, but now I could not. So I couldn't get to my car. I went to the security desk to ask for help and they asked to see the confirmation message on my phone. The guy was so thick it took five minutes to explain that if I could get into my phone I could access the garage and my car!"

"So he let you in to the garage?"

"No. He told me there was nothing he could do. Surely, I said, he could unlock the garage and I could lead him to my car. I had made a note of where it was parked. He could check my license against the registration in the glove compartment to see that it was my car. He said he couldn't leave his desk, and there was nobody else to ask for help. They had cut back on security personnel in favor of CCTVs monitored from a central location in town. And then he added that my license would not help. Paper or plastic identification was useless because it wasn't password secured."

"What am I supposed to do now?" I asked him.

"I don't know," he said. "I'm only following instructions."

"That's when I lost it. You won't help an old lady get to her car?

"No can do," he said.

"Would you run out of here to quell a disturbance in the mall?"

"Of course, that's what I'm paid for."

"I left his office and walked to the middle of the mall, where its two axes meet and there is a little pool and atrium. I stripped, folded my clothes, and put them neatly in my shopping bag, with my shoes alongside. I climbed into the pool and began to sing. I knew I was certain to attract attention."

"And this is when the police came?"

"Yes, that shit – forgive me – that security guard did not come himself but called the police after somebody told him there was a naked woman singing in the pool – and I'm sure I was off-key."

Dr. Segal suppressed a smile as he pictured the scene in his mind's eye. A naked 65 year old woman displaying herself in the pool and attracting attention by singing loudly and badly.

"What were you singing?"

"The first thing that came to mind," she said. "The Star Spangled Banner."

Dr. Segal smiled. "That might be enough to attract the police."

"Oh, it did. They demanded that I get out of the pool and get dressed. I told them I would do this on two conditions. Somebody had to bring me a towel. I wasn't going to get my clothes wet. And the security guard had to let me though the garage door so I could get to my car. A large crowd had gathered by then, some of them were taking pictures or filming the scene with the phones. It must have gone viral because any number of friends told me afterwards that they saw it. Unfortunately, so did my boss – now my former boss."

"Did they bring you a towel?"

"No, the three cops just stood there whispering to one another. It was a standoff. None of them wanted to get wet by coming into the pool after me. While they deliberated I finished the anthem. I only know the first verse. Suddenly, a woman appeared with a towel. She worked in a bath shop and brought it out thinking I would cover myself with it. You may not believe me but I am a very modest person. This was the first time I exposed myself in public but I was desperate and needed to do something dramatic to convince the guard to let me into the garage. I assumed he would be thrilled to do so to end the nuisance I was causing, something that might cost him his job if I continued to sing and attract attention."

"Is this when they arrested you?"

"Yes. I made the mistake of getting out of the pool and trying to dry myself with the towel. Two of the cops grabbed me, wrapped the towel around me, and carried me off. You can see it all on You Tube. My grandson has said nothing but I'm worried that his friends told him about it and that he is embarrassed. It's not what I had in mind for his birthday."

"But the police didn't charge you?"

"I thought you knew? They agreed to let me go – fully dressed, of course – and get access to my car if I agreed to undergo treatment. That's why I'm here."

"Have you learned a lesson from this experience?"

"You bet I have! Passwords are an even bigger nuisance than I thought, the police are out to protect the system, not people, and the Internet is as much a curse as a blessing. The posting on You Tube and other sites cost me my job, but I have had several job offers and even more propositions."

"Propositions, really?"

"You can't believe anyone would find me attractive?"

"That's not what I meant."

"Then what did you mean?"

"Let's continue with your reactions. Mine are unimportant."

"The propositions I ignored, but I'm thinking of accepting an offer to appear nude on a calendar with an anti-technology theme."

The cat stirred again and walked around Dr. Segal's right left. Dr. Segal pushed it away and stood up. "I think we're done for the day, Mrs. Mahoney."

She rose and walked to the door, opened it, and left, followed obediently by her cat.

*

Dr. Segal hoped his second appointment would be less fraught. Ms. Jordan had only recently been admitted and he had met her once. Their discussion had been perfunctory. He hoped she would be receptive to therapy and the new drug he wanted to prescribe in addition to a tranquilizer. His optimism did not last long.

Ms. Jordan was admitted at the request of her employer, a major airline. She was a supervisor with a good record and twelve years of experience. The airline reported that she had walked off her job and may have had a nervous breakdown. She had failed to enter the right password at a critical moment and flight operations at her airport ground to a halt. She denied any responsibility for what had happened, and the airline had given her the choice of therapy or looking elsewhere for employment.

Dr. Segal read out to her the airline's account of what had transpired.

"This is utter nonsense, you know."

"Are you telling me there is no truth to what they say? They are a major airline."

"Surely you didn't come down in the last storm, Doctor. They will say anything they think makes them look good and passes responsibility for a bad outcome on to someone else. In this case, to me."

Dr. Segal wondered if he was dealing with another paranoid.

Ms. Jordan took his silence for an invitation to proceed with her account of what had transpired.

"The computer system had gone down at the airport on my duty shift," she explained. "All flights were delayed, and many were ultimately canceled. I had to rebook passengers on later flights and summoned extra staff to handle the demand. To do all the rebooking efficiently I had to activate a special program on the computer system. I called it up, identified myself by username and password, and was brought to the next prompt that required an additional password, unique to this program."

"So this is where things went wrong?

"Yes and no. I had no problem remembering this unusually long password because I resorted to mnemonics. It began with the three capital letters: MLK. I remember them as Martin Luther King, one of my heroes since childhood. Next came a string of numbers. I broke these down into three sets of four and thought of them as years. I associated them with historical events: Columbus' discovery of America, Pearl Harbor, and the years when Elvis Presley was born and died. You have to wonder about the last two sets. Were they random or was the person who thought them up also a fan of the King? Elvis was followed by an exclamation mark, which is a natural. Then came 34SF11m. I didn't have to puzzle long over that one either, My partner wears size 34 snug jeans – that show off his bottom very nicely – and 11 medium shoes. And finally, there were a string of zeroes ending with a lower-case pt. It's not hard to remember six zeroes – they represent Monday through Friday -- and physical therapy – PT -- is what I need every Saturday in this stressful, chair-ridden job. End of the code, end of the week."

Now it was Dr. Segal's turn to be speechless.

Ms. Jordan continued. "I got lucky with this code They are supposed to change it every three months, but never get around to doing it. They've used the same code for over a year now."

"Shouldn't you have told them about it?"

"Absolutely not. I would have to figure out a new set of mnemonics and that could be a real challenge. And they don't really need to change the password. Think about it. There are two or three people who do my job at our four hubs, so a dozen folks all together. If you can't trust them, who can you trust? If they wanted to shut down the airline they could clear the skies and bring the management to its knees in a matter of hours. As for an outsider doing this they would have to get into a locked room in which there were always people on duty who would know they were intruders and sound an alarm. Hackers would need to know the program existed, and it can only be used to facilitate rebooking. What incentive would they have to do that? It's another example of the absurd lengths businesses go to build firewalls around things that don't need protecting. All they succeed in doing is making life harder for everyone trying to do their job.

"I still don't understand.

"What don't you understand?"

"Why everything went haywire if you had the right password."

"It was a system error. They happen all the time. These are complicated programs with lots of potential to go awry. And one of the things that's almost certain to go wrong is the error message when there is a glitch. The programmers have no idea of what will happen when their programs operate in real time and interface with other programs. Their pre-programmed error messages are hit and miss and, I suspect, designed to direct attention away from possible faults in the program. Better to blame it on the operators, so up comes a message on the screen that reads 'error in username or password.' This is what happened with me and no matter how much I insisted that I had the right password they refused to believe me, the idiots. They believed the error message instead."

"And you threw a fit?"

"No, I tried in a calm voice to explain that it was the program, not me, that needed fixing. I got nowhere. One of the higher-ups arrived, furious at being called away from his dinner and began screaming at me. I realized the situation was hopeless and likely to escalate so I collected my purse and coat and walked out."

"They said it was you who screamed."

"They also claim that my alleged password failure was responsible for the grounding of almost a third of their fleet. Who are you going to believe?"

"I really don't know." Dr. Segal thought her story made a lot of sense but so do those of clever paranoids Their tall tales often appear more logical and credible than the truth.

"Well then, there's little hope for society when educated people like you can be fooled by the lies corporations and governments propagate."

"Surely, they wouldn't go to the extreme of having you committed. I'm sorry, I mean coercing you, as I understand it, to come here for treatment."

"Why wouldn't they? They have no more principles than the people who ran the Soviet Union. They committed dissenters to psychiatric wards to get them out of the way but also to convince themselves and the public that the system was healthy. The dissidents were the healthy ones, and severely punished for it. It was shameful of psychiatrists who swore the Hippocratic oath to play their game."

Without prompting Dr. Segal thought of doctors in Hitler's Germany who had done even worse things to accommodate to the Nazis. But this is twenty-first century America, not Nazi Germany. Still, Ms. Jordan had a point, but only if she was telling the truth and not spinning a web of self-serving lies. Maybe, he told himself, he should withhold judgment for a while.

"So, are you going to play the game or stand up to them?" she asked.

"I'm committed to doing my best for my patients."

"That's part of the problem,"

"What do you mean?"

"As long as you think of us as patients, you've put us in a box and are taking their side."

"I don't think that's fair."

Ms. Jordan looked him in the eye and said nothing.

After a pause that would have been uncomfortable anywhere else but a psychiatrist's consulting room, Dr. Segal asked Ms. Jordan if she wanted to go back to work at the airline.

"Frankly, I'm undecided. The pay is excellent, sometimes the work is interesting, and I like most of my colleagues. But I'm furious at how I have been treated. I'm thinking of looking for a job with another airline. Another possibility is something far-removed from the digital world."

"Wouldn't that be a mistake, given you skills, and the far-reaching tentacles of the information revolution?"

"Quite possibly. But there are many people who are going off-line, not by choice initially, but now happily so. They are rejecting the digital world. There's a movement out there, and who knows where it might lead."

To Dr. Segal this all sounded very Luddite. He looked at his watch, breathed a sigh of relief that the session was coming to an end. Ms. Jordan got the message, rose to her feet, and he escorted her to the door. He returned to his desk to write up notes of the two sessions, which took him some twenty minutes.

Dr. Segal signed off his computer, shut it down, and locked his office door as he left. Feeling a great sense of relief, he walked down the hallway and told himself that in another ten seconds he would be out of the ward. In less than a minute he would leave the hospital, and in two minutes more at most be in his car, drive out of the parking lot and leave this place behind. At the exit to the ward, he reached out with his right hand to punch in the code. He keyed in the numbers without giving it any thought. Nothing happened. He looked over just in time to see a little red light flash off on the keypad.

"That's odd," he thought. He reached out again, more carefully this time, and digit by digit slowly punched in the code. He waited for the expected flash of green light and the metallic click that signaled that the door was now unlocked. Instead, the red light appeared again.

"How can this be," he muttered. I didn't make a mistake. He realized that he had one more try before the system would shut down for some indeterminate period of time. He had to get it right.

GREGOR SAMSA'S SISTER

As Greta woke up she gradually became aware of her body. She had no sensation in her right leg, as the other leg had pressed on it for the last hour. She gently rolled on to her back and pushed away the duvet with her left hand. Her bladder signaled but did not communicate urgency. She relished a few more moments of peace before getting up and facing what she knew would be a busy day. She arched her back, stretched her long legs, and was pleased that she now had feeling back in her right leg. She wiggled her toes.

Her legs, she thought, were her best physical feature. Men eyed them. When circumstances permitted she would play a little game with her admirers. She would reveal a little more leg than was considered proper, men would glance down furtively, and both parties would pretend nothing had happened. She liked her body and felt vindicated in her attachment by its ability to arouse men. Greta never gave much thought to what might happen next because nothing could until she was married. When she thought of men, and one in particular, she experienced a warm feeling that sometimes suffused throughout her body and very occasionally grew strong enough to turn from pleasurable to almost painful.

Greta could linger no longer. She got out of bed in a quick twist and roll and then stretched upwards once her feet were planted firmly on the floor. She dressed and combed her hair. She had it tied in a bun to keep her long black hair from obscuring her face. She wore underwear, bra, slip, skirt, and jersey. She thought of her outer layers as something akin to an insect's carapace that covered and protected her body, even if they somewhat restricted her speed of movement. The bathroom was free so she rushed in to do her morning ablutions.

She was on her way back to her bedroom when she heard a commotion outside her brother's bedroom. Father was knocking on his door.

"Gregor, Gregor," he called out, "what's going on?'

He repeated himself in a deeper and more insistent tone of voice: Gregor! Gregor!"

There was still no reply. Greta moved to the door and knocked lightly.

"Gregor? Are you all right? Do you need anything?'

"I'll be ready right away," Gregor replied.

His father returned to the dining room to resume his breakfast.

In a low and calm voice Greta said: "Gregor, open the door, I beg you."

The door remained closed. Greta waited in vain for it to open or for her brother to say something.

The doorbell to their flat rang and Greta went to see who it was. In the doorway stood the manager of the firm where her brother worked as a salesman. She invited him in and returned to her brother's bedroom door.

"Gregor, the manager is here," she said.

He did not reply. Grete wondered what was going on and why her brother was still in his room at this late hour of the morning. Her mother appeared and knocked loudly against the door.

"He's in there," her mother said. He did not come to breakfast and has not left the flat.

She knocked again and they heard a gargling sound inside.

"He must be sick," her mother exclaimed. "Go to the doctor right away. Hurry to the doctor."

 The manager, who had positioned himself behind the two women, also heard the strange sound. "That sounded like an animal's voice," he said.

Greta's mother began to cry.

"Anna! Anna!" yelled her father from the dining room. He clapped his hands, "Get a locksmith right away!"

Greta and her sister rushed through the hall with swishing skirts, open the door of the apartment, and went down the stairs as quickly as they could.

Once outside, Greta asked Anna what she thought was going on?

"I don't have a clue," she replied.

Gregor's father finally opened the door to his room and he and the manager peered inside. Gregor was nowhere to be seen but there was a very large beetle on the floor. As the door opened they could see it scurry towards them. The manager quickly headed back towards the door of the flat, went through it quickly into the hall. He stretched out hand to grasp the railing of the staircase, as if it would bring him back to the world he knew. He went down the stairs two steps at a time.

Huddled under the bed, Gregor thought "if only my sister had been there! She was clever and fond of him. The manager, this friend of the ladies, would certainly let her calm him down." But his sister had left and Gregor would have to cope for himself.

His mother began to wail, got up from the dining table, and collapsed into the arms of his father, who had rushed towards her.

The manager's flight had completely unnerved Greta's father, who had previously displayed little emotion. The manager had left his cane behind, along with his hat and overcoat, draped over a chair. Greta's father picked up the cane in his right hand and with his left reached out for a large newspaper on the table. Stamping his feet on the floor, shouting, and pointing the tip of the cane at Gregor he drove him back into his room. Gregor tried without success to signal benign intentions by swiveling his head back and forth in what he thought conveyed respectful attitude. His father only grew more agitated and stomped that much harder with his feet. Then his father lashed out at Gregor with the cane and he scurried, now bleeding severely, back into his room. His father slammed the door shut. Suddenly all was quiet.

Greta and Anna had gone their separate ways but before discussing the morning's events. The sisters could not believe that their brother had been transformed into a beetle but it was the only explanation they could come up with.

"But how could such a thing happen?" Anna asked.

"What worries me is that if it could happen to him, it could happen to us," Greta replied.

"No, surely not!"

"Would you have thought yesterday that he could wake up an insect?"

The conversation went no further, and Anna and Greta walked in silence for another few minutes before saying their farewells and going their separate ways to work.

Of the two sisters, Greta was the more thoughtful and also the one with higher aspirations. She loved music and played the violin. She dreamed of studying at the conservatory, but the parents could not afford what they regarded as an indulgence. Her brother was sympathetic and had told her repeatedly that he hoped to move up the ladder in his company and that when this happened, he would pay for her musical studies. In the meantime Greta worked in a bank, initially as a teller, but had recently been promoted to a secretarial position in the back office. There were two eligible men who worked there, one a clerk, the other an assistant to one of the partners. More attractive men, and better catches, came and went on business with the four partners. One had taken notice of her, chatted her up, and invited her for coffee. He was tall, had piercing blue eyes, a trim moustache, and swept back jet-black hair. They discovered a common interest in modern literature and had talked at length about Franz Kafka's *The Trial*. She was hoping he would ask her out again.

When she returned home that evening Greta discovered that her brother had stayed in his room all day as far as anyone knew. She reasoned that the must be hungry. She had no idea what a beetle liked to eat but took it upon herself to bring a bowl of warm, sweet milk into his room. He was still her brother, after all, and his earnings paid for their lodgings. However, he could hardly continue his job in insect form. Perhaps tomorrow he would wake up as himself. Wouldn't that be reassuring for everyone.

Early the next morning when it was still dark and before her parents were up, she crept down the hall, and knocked gently on his door. She waited a moment, then tip-toed in, and looked around. She did not see Gregor at first, but he moved just enough to signal to her that he was under his bed. It was a shock to see him, and she could not prevent herself from fleeing the room and slamming the door shut once she did.

She felt chagrined running off as she did and immediately went back to reopen the door. She entered the room pretending that she was in the presence of a serious invalid. Gregor had pushed his head forward to the edge of the bed and was clearly observing her. She looked down at him and the bowl of milk. She noted with astonishment that the milk was untouched but there were a few droplets spilled around it. She cleaned them up with a rag and took the bowl out of the room. She returned a few minutes later with a tray. She put it down, spread old newspapers on the floor and then took small plates from the tray and laid them down on top of the newspapers The plates contained half-rotten vegetables, bones from the evening meal, covered with a white sauce which had almost solidified, some raisins and almonds, cheese, a slice of dry bread, and some salted bread smeared with butter. She also put down another bowl into which she had poured water. Wondering if Gregor would be restrained about eating in her presence, she went away quickly and even turned the key in the lock so that her brother could make himself as comfortable as he wanted.

Greta tried as far as possible to pretend that she was unfazed by her brother's transformation or her efforts to bring appropriate food to him. She had no inkling of how troubled he was by his inability to speak and thank her. Grete did not understand why he now scurried out of sight whenever she entered the room. One day, about a month after Gregor's transformation, she came into his room a little earlier than usual and found him motionless and staring out the window. She did not know why, but she turned on her heels and left in a hurry. She returned at midday and felt the same sense of ill-ease. She fought off the desire to flee when she saw a little bit of her brother protruding from under the couch. She wondered if Gregor had picked up on her growing anxiety. He made himself increasingly scarce at hours when he expected her. He had somehow carried the bedsheet over to the couch and arranged it so that he could hide underneath. She was amazed at his ability to move the sheet and wondered what she had done to offend him.

For over two weeks Gregor's parents avoided his room. They were full of praise for Grete, a striking reversal of their useful scorn of her. They often waited outside Gregor's bedroom door for Grete to emerge after feeding him or tidying up and report on his condition. They wanted to know what he looked like, whether he had eaten, how he had behaved. Every day, Grete's mother asked if her brother showed any sign of returning to human form. His mother finally screwed up her courage to go into his room but her husband prevented her from doing so.

Gregor remained an insect and had become more adapted to his new body, the range of its possible movements, and what made him feel good. He would spend hours hanging from the ceiling, where he could breathe more easily and swing back and forth, a motion he came to enjoy. Grete became aware of her brother's new form of entertainment. She conspired with her mother to bring her into his room while her husband was away on an errand. She waited until Gregor had come off the ceiling and on to the floor before opening the door to let her enter. Seeing his mother in the doorway, Gregor took refuge under a sheet on the sofa. Mrs. Samsa went through the drawers of her son's dresser, for reasons not obvious to Grete. She stood in place looking at her mother but keeping an eye on the sofa, wondering if Gregor would choose to emerge. Grete had earlier moved the furniture into one corner of the room, sensing that her brother now wanted as much open space as possible. Mrs. Samsa was upset by this arrangement, wanting to keep the room just as it was in expectation of the reappearance of her son in his usual form. She thought that Gregor would also be upset because he was used to his furniture and its arrangement.

"It looks like we are abandoning him," she said to Grete, but also to Gregor, hoping that he would understand what she said. She wanted to communicate that she was not giving up hope for his return. Grete did not agree. She saw herself as Gregor's spokesman and was confident that he valued open space above all else. He needed room to crawl and swing. She remained adamant in the face of her mother's insistence that all the furniture be restored to its original position. Her mother was stunned by her opposition. She went into shock when she finally caught a glimpse of Gregor, who had come out from under the sheet to see if the women were still there.

"*Gott in Himmel!*" she muttered and looked like she was about to collapse. Grete put her arm around her mother to steady her and ushered her from the room. Once in the living room she sat her mother down and ran to get some smelling salts to keep her from fainting. Her father was furious when he returned home and found out what had happened. He grabbed the first thing in sight, which turned out to be apples in a fruit dish on the living room table. He rushed into Gregor's room and discovered him on the floor. He tossed an apple at him, but missed, and Gregor began to scurry away. He threw another, but without much force. It glanced against Gregor's back and did him no harm. The next one hit him squarely on his carapace and lodged in his back. Gregor seemed unable to drag himself away. His mother, only partly dressed, ran into the room, and stumbling over her skirt, collided with her husband. She pleaded with him to stop, which he had, having run out of apples.

They stood motionless staring at the immobile Gregor. Neither of them had the courage to stoop down and remove the apple lodged in his carapace, so it remained there -- for almost a month.

Due to this injury, Gregor lost much of his mobility. He crawled with great difficulty, and it took minutes for him to make his way across the room. He could no longer climb up the walls to the ceiling. His parents felt sorry for what had happened and left the door of his room open every evening. He lay in the darkness of his room, where he could not be seen from the living room. The family wondered if he could understand their conversation. Grete insisted that he could, but her parents were not convinced.

They no longer held the lively discussions of earlier times. All of them were subdued and few words were said about Gregor, a subject that was now close to tabu. After dinner, Grete's father would fall asleep in his chair and her mother would sew fancy underwear for a fashion shop. Grete studied shorthand and French in the hopes of getting a better position in the bank. Sometimes her father would wake up, say a few words to Gregor's mother and then go back to sleep. Grete and her mother would exchange a tired grin. Her sister made herself scarce and hardly spoke to anyone. When the clock sounded ten, Grete's mother would try gently to wake her husband and persuade him to go to bed because he needed to be up at six to go to work. But he had become increasingly obstinate and insisted on staying longer at the table, even though he invariably fell asleep there. She would tug at his sleeve, whisper endearments into his ear, but they had no effect. When he did wake up, he would mutter something like "What a life! I get no peace in my old age!" Ultimately, he would let the three women help him to the bedroom door.

Without Gregor's contribution the household budget had to be tightened. The maid was let go, but the heavy-set, unkempt, and gruff charwoman came every morning to do the heavy work. Grete's mother sold several pieces of jewelry that she and Grete shared on the rare occasions when one or the other dressed up. Her father made some extra money by bringing bank employees their breakfast, and her mother took in washing.

Grete was horrified when her mother asked her to see if the bank would like her to bring them breakfast. She was hoping to move up in the world and being identified as the daughter of an impoverished family would be a mark against her in a status-conscious bank. She shuddered to think about what effect it might have on the handsome customer who took her out for coffee. Her mother was adamant and the family needed money, so she did as instructed in the expectation that the bank manager would politely decline her offer. To her shock, he accepted, and now she had to confront her mother every day at work. She pleaded with her mother to pretend she was not her daughter and to treat her with the same polite deference she did other bank employees. Her mother agreed. Nobody said anything to her, and she hoped that the bank manager had been kind enough to keep her relationship their little secret.

Grete was increasingly focused on life outside her family's apartment. The bank client who had asked her out for coffee invited her to lunch. He took her to an elegant restaurant just off the town's main square. The décor was very traditional but the menu was largely French. The tables were set far enough apart that they could carry on a conversation with little risk of being overheard. Their talk was hardly intimate. It was mostly about books they both enjoyed, and music, once Grete let it be known that she was an aspiring violinist. Herman asked her what she liked playing, and she described her quite different loves for Bach and the Romantic composers. They were both drawn to Bach's seeming simplicity but ability to use it for such complex ends. Herman asked her if she had ever seen Japanese prints, and Grete confessed she had not. He told her that artists like Eisen and Hiroshige did in art what Bach did in music and promised to invite her to his apartment to see his growing collection of their prints. She in turn offered to play a Bach partita for him. The food was excellent. They ate oysters and turbot in a very delicate sauce and enjoyed a half bottle of Sancerre. Grete concentrated more on her partner and their conversation, and her high derived from that more than it did from her glass of wine.

Grete had difficulty concentrating on her work that afternoon. Her thoughts were about Herman, what an interesting, cultured, and attractive man he was, and how she could talk to him in a way she could not with her family or few friends. She had always felt a little stifled by her family, and now that her mother was delivering breakfast to the bank, embarrassed by them. What would Herman think if he discovered that her family had sunk low enough that her mother had to take in washing and look for work outside the house? She hoped he would make allowances, and perhaps appreciate her knowledge and musical talent even more given her background. But then a truly dark thought crossed her mind: what if he learned about her brother? It would be a positive social embarrassment for him to court a woman whose brother was a beetle. She could explain that he had been a normal, even admirable, person before his transformation, but that she could not explain. It had just happened. What if it ran in the family? Or what if he thought it did? Nobody would risk marrying a woman if there was even the remotest chance of waking up one morning and you were in bed with a bug!

At home, Grete became touchy in a way that was quite new for her. Her parents attributed it to having to clean up Gregor's room, a task they had "delegated" to her. She did not mind the chore but did feel the stress of her role of go-between her brother and her parents. They continually asked her how he was, as if she knew. They now lacked all courage to enter his room, which was probably a good thing, she thought, given what had happened last time. She noted how slow the beetle had become, and then berated herself for referring to him as an insect and in the third person instead of as her brother. Gregor never responded to any of her inquiries; he just remained where he was without moving as if she had not opened the door.

One day, early in the morning while a heavy rain struck the windowpanes, she began to speak to him in a normal way again. Gregor started to crawl toward her slowly and seemingly with effort. She reached down to pat him, but he drew back. Grete continued to bring him his meals, but thought less about pleasing him. In the morning, she would hurriedly put a tray of food in his room before rushing off to work. In the evening, she would sweep away what was left with a broom, paying little attention to how much had been eaten. Gregor had all but stopped eating. He might put some into his equivalent of a mouth, possibly leave it there for some time only to spit it out.

Grete still cleared up the room in the evening, making sure to remove what looked like fecal matter to her. She did so quickly and somewhat superficially, leaving the odd stain on the wall and some dust balls.

Grete practiced her violin more than usual, rehearsing her Bach. She was more than ever convinced that the violin was her ticket out of the family flat and its confining and all too predictable life. Her parents would quietly come into the dining room, sit down, and listen. She imagined that Gregor had come closer to his door to do the same. His sister began to play; father and mother paid close attention, one on each side, to the movements of her hands. Grete played beautifully as her left hand moved nimbly over the strings. She approached Bach in a restrained way but still managed to impart emotion to her playing.

The several tenants the Samsa's had taken in also liked to listen to Grete play. But they did not stay long. Once they had realized that they shared the flat with a rather large and mysterious beetle, treated bizarrely like some member of the family, they gave notice. Their departure was abrupt and caused a scene because one of them refused to pay his week's rent.

For Grete, this was a turning point. When her mother had one of her coughing fits, she called her father aside and told him "We have to try and get rid of it. This situation will be the death of both of you, I can see it coming. We can't all work as hard as we have to and then come home to be tortured like this. We can't endure it. I, for one, can't endure it anymore." She started crying and big tears flowed down her cheeks. Her mother wiped them away with a towel and steady hand movements.

"My child," her father said, "what are we to do?

Grete shrugged her shoulders as her previous certainty had given way to helplessness and resignation.

"If he could just understand us," said his father almost as a question. Anna, the younger sister, shook her hand vigorously, while crying, to suggest that it was out of the question.

"If he could only understand us," repeated Gregor's father, "then perhaps we could come to some arrangement with him." He closed his eyes to signal acceptance of his daughter's certainty that it was quite impossible.

"It's got to go," shouted Anna. "It's the only way, Father. You've got to get it out of your head that it's Gregor. We've only harmed ourselves by believing this. It can't be Gregor. If it were, he would have seen how possible it is for human beings to live with a creature like that and he would have left of his own free will. We wouldn't have any more trouble and could carry on with our lives. We would remember him with respect." She rushed over to her father, who had become excited. Her mother lay in her chair with her legs stretched out and pressed against each other, her eyes nearly closed. Grete took a chair next to her father and put her arms around his neck.

When the cleaner came in early in the morning, she woke everyone up as usual. She had been asked not to slam the doors but in her hurry she always did. The cleaning woman had a peek into Gregor's room. At first, she thought he was lying there. She was holding her long broom and tried to tickle Gregor with the handle end from the doorway. He did not move. She grew bolder and poked at him, also with no response. She then pushed him across the floor without meeting any resistance and only then did it dawn on her. She whistled to herself, then shouted in the darkness to the family: "Come and have a look at this thing, it's dead, it's stone dead!"

Mr. and Mrs. Samsa sat upright in their bed struggling to hear what the charwoman was saying. They got up hurriedly, threw enough clothes on to look respectable, and went out to the dining room where Grete had been sleeping ever since the three boarders had arrived. She had not yet moved back to her room. She was fully dressed and all the blood had drained from her face giving her an unearthly pale look.

"Dead?" Mrs. Samsa asked, looking at the charwoman. "That's what I said. Go have a look for yourself." Mrs. Samsa did not move.

"Let's thank God for this," said her husband. He crossed himself, and the three women followed suit. Grete moved to the doorway and was staring at the seemingly dead insect. "Just look how thin he is. He hasn't eaten anything much for so long." Gregor's body was indeed desiccated and almost two dimensional. Grete walked over to him, lifted him gently, and turned him on his back. His multiple little legs were all curled up. There could be no doubt that he was dead.

"Grete, come sit with us in here a little while," said Mrs. Samsa in a soft voice. Grete returned to the dining room. The cleaner shut Gregor's door and opened wide all the dining room windows. The fresh morning air was warmer than usual for the end of March. "It's going to be a lovely day," her father said.

They decided the best way to relax was to go for a walk. They had not only earned a break from work, they were in serious need of one. They sat at the table and quickly wrote three letters: Mr. Samsa to his employers, Mrs. Samsa to her contractor, and Grete to her supervisor. None of them were prepared to acknowledge that their son or brother had died, so each made up their own excuse for not coming to work that day.

The charwoman stood in the doorway with a smile on her face as if she had some good news to report, but would not say what it was until prompted. The almost vertical ostrich feather stuck in her cap, a constant source of irritation to Mr. Samsa, swayed in a direction opposite to the motion of her head. "What do you want then?" Mrs. Samsa asked.

The charwoman smiled. "That thing in there," she pointed toward Gregor's room. "You needn't fret about how you're going to get rid of it. It's all sorted." Mr. Samsa raised his arm to stop from describing in any detail what she had done.

The cleaner got the message. "Cheers, everyone," she announced, turned sharply, and went down the hall to the door. The family could hear her close it on her way out.

"I'm going to fire her," said Mr. Samsa. The rest of the family said nothing. After a minute of silence, Grete rose and walked to one of the open windows. Her mother followed her and put her arms around her. Mr. Samsa twisted round in his chair to look at them. He called out: "Come, let's forget about what has happened. Let's push this old stuff out of our minds. Come and give me a bit of attention." The two women hurried over and kissed him and hugged him.

Not long after they left the flat, arranged for their letters to be delivered by a local messenger, and then boarded one of trams whose terminus was in the rolling hills at the edge of the city. They made themselves as comfortable as they could on the hard but angled wooden seats and directed their attention to city sights and then to the open country and farmland they reached to in about a half-hour. En route they agreed to find a smaller flat, as they no longer needed so many bedrooms. With any luck they could find one that was cheaper but with better access to tram lines. Grete became more animated in the course of their journey. Mr. and Mrs. Samsa were both struck with how their daughter was blossoming into a beautiful young lady. Each read the other's thoughts, which were about finding a good man for her. As soon as they reached their destination Grete was the first to get up and stretch out her young body.

ROUGH WATERS

Henry had booked the trip on-line for himself and his family. It looked legit, even though he had found the company and the references on the dark web. He checked it out on the regular Internet and found seemingly independent sites that suggested it had mostly satisfied customers. The company made all the usual disclaimers about delays due to inclement weather, crossings aborted by coast guard intervention, and refusal to accept any responsibility for what happened once they arrived in North Africa. It was a risky business after all, but Henry was willing to take the chance and had managed to convince his initially reluctant wife that it was the only prospect of their daughters having a good life.

The company promised to supply life vests and fresh water and claimed that more than 90 percent of its crossing had been successful. Only a few ships had turned back or been diverted by Italian or Tunisian authorities. Henry reasoned that whoever ran the operation had a strong interest in successfully ferrying people to their destination. If he failed to do this, people would post unfavorable reviews and the business would go belly up – literally perhaps. It was not a pleasant thought. Henry was old enough to remember watching BBC reports of boat people being rescued in the Med – if they were lucky – by European coastguard and humanitarian ships when their overpacked and unseaworthy tubs run into trouble. These disasters involved Africans trying to get to Europe. Europeans going the other way were richer, more sophisticated, and better organized.

The more serious problem, Henry thought, would be at the other end. Migrants from Europe were not for the most part put in tented camps ringed by barbed wire. Although there were some who argued for such treatment on the grounds of revenge. They were treated politely, transported to hotels they had booked in advance, and given the freedom of the city. They were also shaken down for money. For many migrants, North Africa was only a temporary destination. They were in transit to sub-Saharan Africa. Either way, North African authorities demanded considerable money for either residence or laissez-passer permits. It had become a major source of income for littoral countries, surpassing remittances they received from Europeans of North African origin.

Henry had tried for some months without success to arrange for a quick path to citizenship for himself and his family in an English-speaking African country. He promised to set up a business, employ locals, and benefit the economy. African countries received a multitude of such offers and sold citizenship to the highest bidders. Henry was not in this category. He was comfortably middle class, an executive at a medium size firm with solid experience in marketing. His offer to establish a profitable business was not fully credible. In the absence of a visa he could not board a flight for Africa. The Mediterranean was the only escape route for himself and his family. The alternative, staying in Huddersfield, he considered out of the question.

Charlotte initially thought Henry was losing it. Moving to Africa was not her idea of a better life. She knew many people talked about a bleak future but they had a life here in Huddersfield, and a good one at that. She had grown up in a working-class family and was now comfortably middle class. She was not about to leave on a lick and a promise, and she convinced herself, the naysayers were all exaggerating. The British had always pulled through and would do so again. Her commitment to stay began to wane when her sister and husband left for Australia. He had family in Melbourne and they arranged for visas. Then came the floods and fires. Huddersfield avoided both, but the local and national news carried the stories and the fighting that broke out in their aftermath. The city was nevertheless on edge and a fire, totally unrelated to climate change, turned into an urban riot. Police fought looters, racial tensions rose, and random acts of violence rose dramatically. The turning point for Charlotte came when her daughter and a friend were roughed up by young thugs on their way home from school. They stole her daughter's watch and gave her a black eye.

The drive to Italy was unproblematic but long and exhausting. There were long lines of traffic, accommodations were difficult to book, and food and meals outrageously expensive. Turned away one night from a hotel that had overbooked they spent the night in the car. The young girls slept without difficulty, their parents did not and had to drive ten hours the next day.

Crossing borders was also a problem. The French had all but excluded the English from entering their country and had used their preexisting facilities at Calais to intern those who came across without valid transit visas. There was a grand irony here because London had helped to pay for these facilities in an earlier era to keep illegal immigrants out of the United Kingdom.

Henry and his family had the proper transit papers for France but getting them for Italy proved more difficult. They had to pay a lot for them to the boat company, which provided this service. Altogether, Henry had paid 2,000 Euros for each of their four passages and another 1,000 Euros for transit visas. He could imagine the boat owners and the Italian bureaucrats arguing over how to split this bribe. Henry and his wife Charlotte had racing hearts at the Italian frontier – Schengen was by now history – but were waved through. They had two more days of driving to reach Reggio Calabria, where they would overnight before taking the car ferry to Messina in Sicily.

Henry kept the car radio on for news alerts in case something happened that caused them to deviate from their route. They were fine, but England was not. The United Kingdom had broken up a few years earlier, with first Scotland and then Northern Ireland going their own ways. Wales was considering leaving as well. The rump state of England was in great disarray. The recession was deepening and threatening to become a recession. Violence was on the rise, much of it directed, as always, against immigrants and minorities, but also against the government. The Tory government had promulgated a set of rules for dealing with the emergency, rules they changed regularly to everyone's annoyance and confusion. But certain prohibitions were constant but regularly broken by individual ministers. The prime minister refused to discipline his cabinet. It leaked out that three ministers, including the Chancellor, had made arrangements to emigrate with their families. The most egregious exposure was of the Defence Secretary who appeared to have transferred important military assets to Australia in return for citizenship for himself and his extended family of twelve.

People did not take kindly to this double standard. Several local Tory offices were torched or broken into and trashed. A former prime minister, who proclaimed his intention to relocate to the Caribbean, was roughed up by protestors before being rescued by the police. Shots were fired at a cavalcade carrying the current prime minister, wounding a bystander. In a well-read *Guardian* piece, a columnist known for her biting wit, compared the behavior of upper-class passengers on the *Titanic* to their present-day counterparts. It was a myth, propagated by publicists for the well-heeled, that women and children were evacuated first from this sinking ship. In practice, the men mostly tried to save themselves and few lifeboats were left for those who had not traveled first class. There was no chivalry at sea, as there was none when the seas threatened to overwhelm the island of Britain. The columnist cited LaRochefoucauld who described hypocrisy as the homage vice pays to virtue. Self-interest had become so blatant among the privileged classes, she observed, that hypocrisy was no longer necessary.

"I'm glad we're leaving," Charlotte said after listening to the BBC news. "It's not the country I grew up in."

"I'm afraid it is," Henry said. "We just turned a blind eye, dismissing this kind of behavior as unacceptable and abnormal. We're the abnormal ones in our commitment to more traditional values."

The BBC news concluded with its daily weather report which these days included an update on the Atlantic Ocean. For the tenth day in a row, and 150 days of the last two hundred, the temperature of the water was more than four degrees below average. The Gulf Stream no longer reached Europe. It had not for some two years now. Instead, the Bear and Spitzbergen currents flowed from the Arctic south to blanket the British Isles. They were rapidly cooling not only Britain and Norway but most of northern Europe, which for millennia had depended on the warming waters of the Gulf Stream. It formerly flowed at an average speed of three knots per hour, was sixty miles broad, a hundred fathoms deep, and its water started north with an average temperature of 50 degrees. It followed the American continent north until it met the Labrador Current and then turned east toward Western Europe.

The news was followed by a discussion, a debate really, pitting a respected climate scientist against a Tory politician who was head of the Climate Research Group.

"Do you want to hear it, or should I turn it off?" Henry asked his wife.

"Let's listen for a few minutes. Otherwise, I'll concentrate on how slowly the traffic is moving."

The climate scientist began by noting how their models were only roughly accurate and at best established a range in which change would occur. The

Tory MP lit into him: "If your models are guesswork you have no right frightening people and even provoking them to violence."

"Our models are not guesswork. Climate change is real. People have a right to know. In any case, scientists don't provoke violence. Politicians do."

"Is that so? First you predicted that the world was heating up. Now you say it is cooling down and that the glaciers will return. This is all nonsense. Our studies suggest that cooling will benefit the British economy."

The scientists tried to stay on point and describe some of the complexity of climate change "The world is heating up due to carbon and methane emissions caused by human machines and farms. But it is uneven. Some parts of the world are getting colder, and all of northern Europe will be covered by glaciers within a century or so because the Gulf Stream no longer warms us. Hotter Atlantic waters have slowed down the Gulf Stream, then stopped it from flowing across to Europe. Now, it doubles back to the Caribbean, making us colder and bringing serious flooding to the US east coast."

"Glaciers move an inch or two a year. The Climate Research Group calculates that it would take at least a million years for them to cause any problem."

"If I'm not mistaken, this the same group that under a different name calculated that Brexit would be a boon to the British economy?"

"Please turn it off," Charlotte said. "I'd rather watch the traffic. I'm now thinking that all this carbon emission might be a good thing if it slows down the glaciers."

"You don't really believe that?"

"No, but it is a comforting thought."

The girls were surprisingly good travelers. Henry and Charlotte stopped every few hours to let them run about. They let them order pizza for lunch and have ice cream later in the afternoon. Charlotte told them they were on a big adventure. They were on their way to a new home that would be warmer and where they could swim all year long.

"Will we have a swimming pool?" her daughter Olivia asked.

"Wouldn't that be nice," Charlotte said.

"Would you like to swim with me before or after breakfast?" she asked Olivia.

"I'd have to get up really early. Could we do it after school? And could I bring a friend?"

"Of course, dear,

"Are we there yet, mummy?" Olivia asked.

"I'm afraid not dear".

"I have to make pee-pee," four year old Emma announced.

"OK, darling, daddy will pull over."

They reached the Tuscany-Umbrian border and overnighted in an undistinguished hotel in an undistinguished town that had the advantage of being just off the motorway. Charlotte convinced both girls to have spaghetti Bolognese instead of another pizza. Their parents were more adventurous and shared some ravioli made with allegedly wild mushrooms and then \a cutlet. They washed it down with a good local red, a Montepulciano.

"Meat will soon be something of the past," Charlotte said. Henry agreed, and wondered if they should feel lucky or guilty about eating it now.

"Lucky, I think. And luckier still to be escaping England. It's only going to get worse."

"I'm afraid you're right. Holland and Scandinavia are more threatened by high waters or cold temperatures, but they've dealt with it better. And then there's Ireland."

"Clever buggers they are. You can't help but admire the Irish, arranging for their entire population to emigrate to America over the next twenty years. They've got lots of support in congress, let alone in the White House."

"And it didn't hurt to send the Book of Kells to the Library of Congress on permanent loan."

The next day's drive was difficult because of the bad weather. It made for stressful driving even though it was all motorway and not so trafficked once they got south of Naples. They had been so exhausted the night before that they and the girls slept later than usual. They had time to do their email but not their normal perusal of the newspaper. Charlotte checked out a few stories on-line on her phone and read them aloud to Henry as he drove. They decided to listen to the BBC news but not any discussion that followed it.

The big news of the day, new demonstrations and violence aside, was the decision by Cambridge and Oxford to relocate to the US. Cambridge was going to someplace called the Upper Valley in Vermont and New Hampshire, where the two states, with federal backing, had made an offer the vice chancellor said she could not spurn. Oxford was moving to New Jersey. The prime minister was apparently blindsided by the news and insisted that King's College Cambridge would not be allowed to remove and take the stained-glass windows from its cathedral to put into an American replica. St. Paul's School in London was relocating to Washington, D.C. The Archbishop of Canterbury insisted that he and other members of the ministry would remain in the country as long as there were English people who needed them.

"In that case," Henry said, "they could leave now."

They arrived more or less on time in Reggio, had another early night, and took the ferry the next morning across the Strait of Messina. They then drove south to Catania and then southwest to the small seaport city of Licata. It was settled by the ancient Greeks, later ruled by Romans, Arabs, and Angevins, and Bourbons. The allies landed there in 1943, doing a lot of damage to the town. It was the setting for John Hersey's famous novel, *A Bell for Adano*. Charlotte filled Henry in on the history when it was his turn to drive. Sightseeing was not on the agenda.

They finally arrived at their destination and checked in at their little albergo. As previously instructed, they went to the Café Grangela, and gave their names to the proprietor. They bought ice cream for the girls and coffee for themselves. Some twenty minutes later a Signor Rossi arrived and joined them at their table. He assured them that their departure would take place as scheduled at 5 am the following morning. Someone would collect them and their belongings at the albergo. He took their car keys and had them sign over the ownership papers. He told them that he would, as agreed, be depositing the sum they had settled on for the sale of the car as soon as he had it inspected. Henry worried that he could just walk off with the car but could not see any way of preventing it. He had no choice but to trust Sr. Rossi. He did not feel at all good about it.

The kids slept well but Charlotte and Henry were up most of the night. They dragged themselves out of bed, woke the kids, and went downstairs. A man named Salvatore introduced himself and told them they were waiting for several more people. He turned on the lights and the coffee machine, put on an apron, and made them unexpectedly good cappuccini. By now four other people had arrived, also interested in some coffee. He returned from the kitchen with milk and biscuits for the girls and in halting English asked their names.

All eight people followed Salvatore on foot to the waterfront and to a boathouse with large doors and corrugated metal sides. Inside, they encountered another ten people. There were two English couples, one of them formed by two middle-aged men. Four others were speaking what appeared to be Flemish or Dutch. The remaining two people were young men who seemed to be crew. The passengers had been told to come with no more than 25 kilograms of belongings per person, packed in something water-tight. The two crew members collected the luggage and told everyone it would be stowed on the boat. They distributed life vests, including small ones for the girls. Charlotte had brought her own, which were the best available for kids, and two for herself and Henry. Two more young men arrived with pastries and coffee and almost everyone indulged. The group was told that, as promised, they would provide a meal during the crossing.

Henry was impressed by the operation until they were escorted out to the dock and approached the ship. It was nothing like those sleek, modern vessels in the on-line brochure. It was an old, wooden hulled fishing boat that did not look all that seaworthy. There was only a small cabin for the skipper and a couple of crew, which meant that passengers would have to stay on the deck where they would be exposed to the elements.

"Surely that's not our boat?" Henry asked Salvatore.

"Yes, it is."

"It's nothing like the ships you advertised."

"It's what's here and what we are using today."

Henry was not the only upset passenger. Several joined him in demanding to speak to whoever was in charge. Salvatore was not initially responsive but finally made a call on his mobile when most of the group insisted they were not boarding that tub or doing anything else until his boss made an appearance. Close to thirty minutes elapsed before a late model Alfa Giulietta appeared. A very tanned and sportily dressed middle-aged man in dark glasses emerged and spoke in Italian to Salvatore.

He then turned to the group and explained in passable English that their two principal ships were in use and this was the only other boat he could press into service today.

"Then we will wait until tomorrow," one of the Flemings or Dutch said.

"That won't be possible," the man in sunglasses said. "Those ships are booked tomorrow and this is what is going out today."

"I said we will wait until tomorrow," the man repeated.

"You can wait as long as you like," signor sunglasses said. "Tomorrow's ships are fully booked. There's no room for you unless some people don't show up, and that is unlikely."

"And why is that?" someone else asked.

"Everyone from northern Europe is anxious to escape. I turn people away every day."

"Surely, you can fit eight more people on one of your ships."

"I can't and I won't. We book to legal capacity, and I don't want to get into trouble."

"You're in trouble with us," someone else shouted. "You took good money for a passage on a seaworthy vessel and now you want to send us across the Mediterranean on this aged fishing boat." There were murmurs of support from the group.

"I understand you are unhappy," signor sunglasses said. "And I will make you an offer. First, let me assure you that this old fishing boat is completely seaworthy. It has fished in these waters for many years without a problem. It has a solid hull and is only slightly slower than the bigger ships. Best of all, the sea today is calm, the crossing will be some six hours, and if we leave now, you will be in port by mid-afternoon. Tomorrow and for two more days the weather will be bad. My regular ships can make it across, but the passage won't be pleasant."`

"What is your offer?" Henry asked.

"I will refund half the cost of your passage."

Discussion ensued among the passengers and most seemed willing to accept the deal. Henry asked how they would know if actually honored his commitment. Mr. Sunglasses thought for a moment, held up his hand for silence, pulled out his mobile and made a telephone call. He then explained to the group that he had awakened his banker who promised to do the transfers as soon as he got to work. "That's the best I can do," he said. "The alternative is to hang around and wait for no-shows and that could be some time. I can't predict."

Henry and Charlotte walked a short distance back from the pier to consult. They didn't like the boat but felt reassured by what Signor Sunglasses had said. They wanted to leave today and did not want to face the uncertainty that refusing this passage would create. The weather was lovely and a smooth crossing would be much easier for the girls. "Even if we don't get half the money back," Charlotte said, "we will still get to Africa."

The gay couple decided to wait for a larger ship and have a little holiday in Sicily in the interim. Everyone else accepted the offer and their luggage was loaded into the hold and they were invited on board. One of the crew motioned to Charlotte and explained to her in a mix of Italian and English that it would be safer for the girls in the cabin. Charlotte could come inside too.

The sun had already risen when they pulled away from the dock. They made their way past the rock barrier on their port side until they were in the open sea. The water was calm and there was only the gentlest of swells. Charlotte went into the cabin with two loudly protesting girls in tow. Henry stayed on deck and chatted up the other English couple. It soon became uncomfortable on deck because of the heat and passengers sought cover under the tarp the crew had slung across the ship forward of the cabin. They altered course and were now running abeam of the swells rather than into them. The ship rose and fell and swayed to one side or another. Several of the passengers found the motion uncomfortable, including one who had previously put on an anti-seasickness patch. Charlotte and the girls were unaffected, as Henry found out when he went inside to check on them. Boredom soon set in except for those struggling with the motion of the ship.

All ships underway are required to have their transponders on at all times. Unknown to the passengers theirs was traveling black to stay undetected because it was not licensed to carry passengers. For the same reason their sonar was not turned on. This put everyone at risk because they were crossing busy sea lanes plied by giant tankers and cargo ships. All these vessels had good, active radar, sonar, and computer programs that warned the bridge of ships in their path. Any collision would be fatal for a smaller vessel, as would passing too close in their wakes. The crew was not worried because the visibility was good, and they periodically scanned the horizon with their binoculars. Mostly, they were on the lookout for coast guard and naval vessels that might intercept them. Their number had increased as the trade in illegal crossings of the Mediterranean had become routine. The crew knew they would have no trouble leaving port because all the local officials had been paid off. The risk of interception increased once they were out of Italian coastal waters. Coast Guard and naval vessels also avoided the busy commercial sea lanes unless they had a special mission that brought them there. Knowing this, the fishing boat headed out into one of the busiest waterways to keep it out of sight.

Fog or haze can develop very quickly at sea with little or no advance warning. This happened at lunchtime when everyone – the odd queasy stomach aside – was munching on sandwiches provided by the crew and drinking bottled water. Most people were feeling relaxed now that they had reached the halfway point of their crossing. As the fog thickened the swell increased and the temperature dropped. Their vessel maintained its speed and the captain turned on its searchlight. This had little effect, as expected, and he cut the light. He also slowed down but it was too late. The fishing boat plowed into some low, unforeseen object. There was a crunching noise as it penetrated their hull. Their sudden loss of weight and buckling of the deck threw passengers overboard, or worse, into the cabin wall or a bulkhead. Moments later the vessel and those in the water were hit by the wake of a large ship. Water washed over the damaged fishing boat because its prow was at the waterline and could not rise over the wave. The remaining passengers and crew were carried overboard, and many were quickly separated from their vessel and one another by the successive, if now receding, wakes.

Charlotte and her daughters were lucky. Charlotte was pushed hard against the wall of the cabin on which she was already leaning and then flung forward. She collided with a crew member, not a railing or wall, and was bruised and stunned, but not badly injured. The two girls were sleeping on a mat beneath her and were tossed about. They were young, had been totally relaxed, and were uninjured despite their encounters with the sides of the wheelhouse. Charlotte gathered them up once she collected her own wits. Her next thought was about Henry, who was nowhere to be seen. Looking through the smashed wheelhouse windows she could see no passengers on deck, and only some of the deck as the rest was under water. She realized the boat was sinking and knew she needed to get off and away before it dragged her and the girls under. She pushed the still dazed girls out of the wheelhouse; its door had been sheared off and was lying at the back of the boat, most of it overboard. She somehow managed to get the girls to the door, pushed them on top of it, then climbed on herself and with a heave pushed it away from the boat. This was not hard to do as the fishing boat was gradually sinking and the door about to float free.

The last of the waves generated by the big ship had passed and the sea had calmed down. Charlotte made the girls hang on to the rope that ran across the door and was previously used to open it from the inside. She lay down and paddled, moving the door away from the boat and looking out for Henry. It was hard to see anything much in the fog; visibility was limited to about ten feet. She shouted out his name but received no reply. She saw no other passengers, which was not a good sign. She told herself that Henry was safe and would find them. She continued to shout his name, as did the elder of the two girls. Charlotte flashed Olivia a big smile.

"Daddy will find us," she assured both girls. "Let's shout out his name together every half-minute." To her amazement, her watch was still working, not that she really intended to be precise about when the called out for Henry. It was the only thing they could do to find him, other than keeping their eyes peeled, and, she thought, it would give the girls something to concentrate on. Someone loomed into view and Charlotte paddled in its direction. To her horror, it was a man's body gently rising and falling on the swell. She had the girls look away, but they had already seen it.

"Daddy! Daddy!" Emma shouted. Charlotte and Olivia looked behind them and there was Henry swimming slowly towards them. Tears came into Charlotte's eyes. She quickly brushed them away and paddled hard on one side of the door to turn it in her husband's direction. Paddler and swimmer quickly closed the distance and Henry reached out to rest himself against the door. This was more weight than the door could stand and it angled sharply with the end Henry was holding on to sinking below the water. Emma would have rolled off if Charlotte and Olivia had not caught her. Henry eased off the door, treading water and holding the edge of the door only with his fingers. The door righted itself.

"This is not going to work," Henry said. "I'll sink the three of you if I put any of my weight on this board."

"What are you going to do?" Charlotte asked.

"Let me find another piece of wreckage that will support me and paddle back on it."

"How will you know where we are?" Charlotte asked

"Do what you did before." Give me a few minutes to scout around and then shout out every minute so I can find you."

"What if you don't find another board?"

"I will."

"Lean over and kiss me,"

Charlotte eased forward on the board until her face was close to his. Henry raised his head, kissed her, smiled at the girls, and swam off into the mist.

Charlotte looked at her watch this time and waited for a minute to pass. It seemed like an eternity. She counted down aloud and at the end of a minute the three of them shouted "Henry" in unison. There was no reply, but she really didn't expect one so soon. They kept shouting every thirty seconds until they grew hoarse. Charlotte insisted that they continue doing so but was losing hope.

"Maybe daddy found a good board or even a raft," she told the girls "but we have drifted too far apart for him to reach us."

"I hope it has water aboard. I'm getting thirsty," said Olivia.

"Me too, mommy," said Emma.

Charlotte was struck by how quiet everything became. The only sound was made by trickles of water coming off the board when its position shifted in the gentle rise and fall of the sea. "How peaceful everything is," she thought.

Postscript

The day I finished writing this story, 23 August 2021, the Associated Press reported that a boat crowded with dozens of migrants capsized off Libya, and at least seventeen people were presumed dead. It was only the latest disaster in the Mediterranean Sea involving migrants seeking a better life in Europe. In August alone, some eighty migrants were presumed dead in two separate shipwrecks off Libya's coast.

LOOKING EAST

The fog rolled in with the fast-moving tide and soon shrouded all of Passamaquoddy Bay. The little port town of Lubec, population 1359, was engulfed as well. The fog was so thick in front of the *Quoddy Tides* that John Cross, its editor, could not see across the road to the general store where residents came to shop and gossip. He imagined the fog thicker still inside the store. The pandemic had led to all kinds of irrational behavior, including a run on items like frozen foods and toilet paper, as people feared, despite assurances to the contrary, that there would be no shortages. There had been scuffles among customers attempting to snatch the last of something from a shelf or display case and complaints that hoarders were leaving nothing for others. The politicization of the virus, and then the election campaign, further divided residents.

In Lubec, everyone knew everyone else, and were often related to them. Even so, people did their best to avoid political discussions. They pretended that all was well, that they were a tight-knit community, that the election was out there and Lubec was here. As the town was toward the end of a peninsula at the eastern end of a state that was the easternmost one of the nation, residents always had a sense of isolation and solidarity. They had largely succeeded in avoiding gun violence and drugs so why not politics? Guns, opiates, and grand larceny were other people's problems. However, politics, like the COVID virus, could not be kept at an arm's length and locals were soon infected by both. The virus proved the easier challenge, at least at the outset. Some elderly people died, some people of all ages were hospitalized, and most donned masks and kept their social distance. Schools and some businesses closed, and many families locked down as far as was feasible.

The pandemic might have been expected to enhance local solidarity, with people helping their neighbors and generally looking after one another. Instead, it intensified divisions and made them more visible. Following Trump, Fox News, and conspiracy theories spread on the Internet, a vocal minority denied the severity of the virus, refused to wear masks or social distance, and opposed all restrictions on commercial activities and individual freedoms. Many of them refused to get vaccinated when this became possible. This politicization divided families and neighbors. The "live and let live" attitude to life, a cherished feature of Down East culture, was seriously threatened. People confronted difficult trade-offs. Do you let a neighbor or delivery man in your house or store if he is unmasked and unvaccinated? Should town meetings be held on-line or in person? Should the town impose a mask mandate? Do I shop at a store owned by a friend if it does not have good ventilation?

Lubec was divided on these questions, as it would be when it came time to vote in November. Biden carried the town and surrounding area by a slim majority. By then, the social fabric of the community was in tatters. In the six months between the onset of the pandemic and the election Lubec began to resemble some town in Northern Ireland, Cyprus, or the Balkans, where members of opposing religions or ethnic groups live cheek-to-jowl, consider the "other" the enemy, but observe the minimal courtesies necessary to maintain the peace. Violence not infrequently breaks out, sometimes triggered by some dispute that was not political or due to the intervention of outsiders intent on stirring up trouble. Lubec avoided violence, but it was a close thing. And all the more so, as a significant percentage of townsfolk went around armed, and not only in hunting season.

*

Sam Stokes, the owner of the general store, was the scion of a family that had lived in the area almost since Lubec was settled in 1811. His ancestors on his maternal side had been German immigrants from the Baltic and he wondered if they were drawn to Lubec because it was named after the Hanseatic city of Lübeck. It was more likely, his wife Marie insisted, that they arrived in pursuit of a fast buck as they began smuggling gypsum, an activity that contributed as much to the town's economy in the nineteenth century as fishing and agriculture.

Sam was related to most of the town and one of the regular activities in the general store was figuring out how he and customers were connected. There was no cracker barrel: the standard catalyst of such discussions in the old days. Nor were there chairs placed near a roaring stove in the winter. People today also had less time to devote to conversation, but Lubec was still a largely cash economy so there was time to talk to Sam when you paid for your purchases. The conversation often lasted longer if nobody else was waiting, and even then, it might continue with the next customer joining in. Genealogical discussions were usually inspired by the birth of a baby. Everyone would claim a connection, often multiple connections, and the newborn was showered with gifts from across the town.

The pandemic put a damper on diaper discussions. Those who took the virus seriously were not about to hang around in a store that was poorly ventilated and where almost half the customers were unmasked. Sam was one of the citizens who urged the select board to impose a mask mandate. The town was divided and the discussion so intense that the select board refused to allow the matter to come up for a vote. This was a clever ploy because they knew the state was about to impose a mandate. Once this happened the town would have to enforce it, but the board could finesse any responsibility. The problem was not so easily resolved because Trump supporters refused to wear masks, claiming they were unnecessary and an infringement on their personal freedom.

Sam was an easy going fellow, but not on this issue. His wife suffered from asthma, putting her at serious risk if he contracted COVID. He tried to explain this to one of his customers who entered the store without a mask and refused to don the one offered to him. Invoking the usual medical justifications got Sam nowhere. The customer dismissed the virus as no big deal and masks as injurious to one's health. "It's no worse than the flu," he insisted. "And it's an unacceptable infringement on my freedom."

"Do you run stop signs at red lights?" Sam asked.

"Why would I do that?"

"Aren't they infringements on your freedom?"

The customer did not reply.

"Of course, you don't run red lights. You're a responsible driver and don't want to hit another car or maybe kill some pedestrian. Wearing a mask is no different."

The customer left the shop without making a purchase.

The following afternoon a different customer entered the store wearing a Trump cap and no mask. Sam asked him politely to don one and he refused.

Another customer intervened.

"Come on Ron," he said. "Put a mask on if only as a sign of respect."

"I respect the Constitution. It's against the law to require mask wearing."

"I won't argue the law with you," the other customer said. "Cover you face to protect your friends and neighbors. Do it voluntarily."

Ron glared at him. With his right hand he pushed his open leather jacket aside to expose a gun with a big black handle lodged in a holster. He put his hand over the grip and looked the other customer in the eye.

"Are you threatening me?"

"Just exercising my constitutional right to bear arms."

"Does it also fire blanks?"

Ron removed his hand from the gun turned around and stormed out of the store.

Sam waited until he had gone to shake his head and smile. "That was below the belt, so to speak."

"He asked for it," the customer said. "I'm sorry Ron and his wife couldn't have kids, but he has no right threaten me that way. Anyway, the baby they adopted has turned into a lovely girl."

*

The story quickly made the rounds and people were divided in their response. For some it was more evidence that the community was at risk. For others it was merely confusing as the accounts they heard were so contradictory. Sam was asked by multiple people to tell them what went down but shook his head and suggested that it would be best to forget all about it.

Robin had only recently turned fifteen. She was an only child, a sophomore in high school, a good student, and looking forward to escaping Lubec for the University of Maine in Orono in two years' time. She was tall and lithe, a good athlete, and a good dancer. What she enjoyed most on the dance floor was the control she had learned to exercise over her body and how to use it to exploit or defy centrifugal force and gravity. She was in touch with the universe when she danced, which she admitted to herself sounded more than a bit arrogant, but it was how she felt. Unlike some of her peers she was not boy crazy but neither was she immune to the hormones that were transforming her from a girl into a woman. Her long-standing friendship with one of the neighborhood boys had gradually morphed into something else.

Robin retained vivid memories of the day it happened. They were part of a group of friends that went whale watching in Quoddy Head State Park. It was early June, a good time for seeing whales off the New England coast, and the local paper had published photographs of a pod taken the day before. It was a warm sunny day, but chilly in the Park because it was on a windswept headland. The group of five split up so they could scan more of the sea with the intention of shouting to the others if they spotted a whale. Robin and Adam went to the far side of the light house and sat down together. Adam put his arm around her and without thinking she snuggled up against him. Her heartrate quickened when Adam tightened his grip on her shoulder. Neither said a word. Robin wondered where this was heading, half-hoping that Adam might kiss her. He made no move to do so she turned her face toward him. He responded in kind and they looked at one another for a moment until Adam, feeling more courageous, drew her too him and kissed her.

They saw no whales but returned to the others holding hands. Nobody said anything but everyone recognized that they were now a couple. Having known each other since childhood their intimacy, although novel, seemed quite natural to them. For all the usual reasons they did their best to keep their parents in the dark. There was an additional concern in their case. Robin's father, Ron Sweeney, was a dyed-in-the-wool Trump supporter. Her mother was not, but she was afraid to voice a contrary opinion. Ron had never hit her but angered easily. Adam grew up in a family of liberal Democrats. Since the beginning of the pandemic Robin's dad had come to loath Adam's.

*

Ron Sweeny was the customer who caused the scene in the general store. He was still fuming about what had gone down and how so many people in the town were taken in by the Democrats who had blown this virus thing all out of proportion, all to turn people away from the President. This made him an even bigger supporter. He asked Republican campaign officials to place a big Trump sign in his front yard and often wore a "Lock Her Up" T-Shirt and always a MAGA cap. Some folks gave him a warm greeting, even a clap on the back. Others avoided him. Some even crossed the street so they would not have to say hello or snub him if they passed close by. Many felt it inappropriate to be so in-your-face about your politics. Democrats found his "Lock Her Up" T-shirt offensive.

Ron felt a great sense of pride and even importance when he strode into the general store. He received a nod of greeting from Sam until the day the state's mask ordinance went into effect. "I'm sorry," Sam said, "you can't come in without a mask on."

"Says who?"

"Says the governor."

"Over my dead body."

"That's what she's trying to prevent."

The conversation went nowhere. Ron left without making a purchase. He drove to a supermarket at the edge of town where he met the same response. He ignored the pleas to put on a mask, filled his shopping cart, and stood in the checkout queue. He stood right behind the person in line in front of him and was asked by the cashier to move back six feet to maintain social distance. He stood his ground. She called the manager, who asked him politely to move back and to wear a mask the next time he entered the store. Ron was considering how to respond when the cashier finished checking out the woman in front of him, making the social distance issue moot. He moved forward and began taking items from his cart and putting them on the conveyor belt. The manager walked off.

The political divide largely, but not entirely, pitted people in town against those who lived in surrounding areas. Both were represented on the select and school boards and they became centers of confrontation. Masks were the initial issue, then school closings and teaching on-line rather than in-person. Mayor Escalus and the police chief also confronted a challenge, initially from Trump supporters who wanted to hold a rally in the center of

town, in front of both the newspaper and general store. They were denied
a permit on health grounds as they refused to wear masks or to maintain
social distance. The Mayor tried to negotiate a compromise: a small number
of Trump supporters could gather and hold up any banners they wanted if
they stood six feet apart. Over Ron's objections, they accepted his offer and
planned an all-day vigil. Different Republicans would take turns standing
in the square in front of a huge "Make America Great Again" banner.

*

Needless to say, the fog rolled in well before the rally began and remained
most of the day. The rally was a bust and the fog prevented the *Quoddy
Tides* from getting good enough photos to publish. Republicans took this
as a deliberate affront and wrote letters to the editor complaining about
liberal censorship, a couple of which were published. John Cross penned an
editorial accusing Republicans of trying to impose their views of everything
from abortion, taxes, and immigration to health and school bathrooms
while complaining about being a marginalized minority. Aggression and
victimhood was a volatile mix and it did not take much provocation to
produce nasty incidents.

Democrats began to display "Biden Harris" signs on their lawns or in
their windows after the Democratic convention in August. Some put
bumper stickers on the cars, as Republicans had already had as Trump's
renomination was a foregone conclusion. Some liberal Democrats also put
up "Black Lives Matter" placards. Biden-Harris signs began to disappear
or were defaced. So did all four of the "Black Lives Matter" placards. Lubec
was almost lily-white. African-Americans making up only one percent of
the population, Hispanics another percent. There was also a hand-full of
Native-Americans and Asians. The "Black Lives Matter" placards were
displayed by a couple of African-American families but also by liberal
Democrats. Those who removed these placards in the middle of the night
were not content with making political statements. They slashed the tires of
the cars in the driveway of two Democrats.

The police were called and the newspaper carried the story on its front page.
Everybody suspected who the culprits were but there was no evidence. A
stakeout on subsequent nights led to the arrest of two teenagers for stealing

Biden-Harris signs but they insisted, and the police believed them, that they had not committing any vandalism.

Other signs of tension were evident. Democrats and Republicans talked to one another even less than before. Democrats were getting vaccinated, and Republicans were not. Democrats gave wide birth to two middle-aged white Republicans who had ridden their Harley-Davidsons in August to Sturgis, South Dakota for the annual motorcycle rally. The Center for Disease Control and the liberal media had warned that it could turn into a super-spreader event, which it did. Both of the local cyclists came down with COVID and one was in the hospital and seriously ill. The positivity rate in town shot up in the weeks after their return. An elderly couple had already died of the virus and one more person succumbed among those infected in what locals now called the Vinnie Virus. Vinnie was the first name of one of the motorcyclists. The tragedy was aggravated by the new hospital protocol of keeping COVID patients isolated so all three patients died without any comfort or farewells from their families.

*

Robin's dad, Alex Zarchy, was an internist and worked nearly around the clock once COVID reached Lubec. He also gave a few public talks to explain to people why the virus was worse than the flu, why they should wear masks and maintain social distance, and later, why they should get vaccinated. By August, vaccines were widely available, but only slightly more than half of the town's adults availed themselves of the opportunity. Following Trump, Fox News, and Internet conspiracy theories, local Republicans spurned the vaccine. Ron Sweeny was a co-signer of a letter to the *Quoddy Tides* claiming that the vaccine might even make you homosexual. The editor thought it appropriate to publish the letter but also a commentary by Dr. Zarchy dismissing the claim and urging people to get jabs. Ron took his reply as a personal affront. He wrote another letter to the paper accusing the doctor of spreading lies and libeling Trump for describing his recommendation to take hydroxychloroquine as ineffective and dangerous. John Cross refused to publish it, even when pressured by other Republicans.

Ron Sweeny became a laughingstock among Democrats, but also a fearsome figure. He was widely assumed to have been the perpetrator of the sign removals and tire slashing. Alex Zarchy was loathed by Republicans. He personified the establishment they so hated and all the more so as he did his best to take the mickey out of them and their preposterous claims about COVID. They resented his education, wealth, and self-confidence. One of them threw a brick one night through one of the windows of his office, which immediately set off an alarm. A police cruiser happened to be close by, saw the presumed perpetrator running away, followed, and arrested him. The cop's tackle of the fleeing suspect was captured by a neighbor on his phone and went viral on the Internet. Out on bail, the alleged perpetrator was interviewed by Fox News, who paid for his defense attorney. He was hailed as a hero by the right but treated as a criminal by the local district attorney. He copped a plea and agreed to pay for the broken window and perform one hundred hours of community service.

*

Robin and Adam could not meet in either of their homes. Ron would go ballistic if he found out that Dr. Zarchy's son had crossed his threshold and was involved with his daughter. First romances are always difficult for fathers of daughters, but all the more where the father was so controlling and so opposed to her beau's family on political grounds.

The young couple's social life was anchored in their group of friends. They were occasionally teased, not about their relationship, but about the non-relationship between their families. They had all read the relevant Shakespeare play in school the previous term and behind their back their friends began referring to them as Romeo and Juliet. Being part of a group gave Robin and Adam a certain anonymity and security. They could see each other but not date openly. They arranged furtive encounters. Jones Beach on Quoddy Head and the State Park were good venues. They were within bicycle range, few locals went to the Beach, and there were woods and open spaces between the beach and light house. They would bike separately to each rendezvous. They enjoyed this subterfuge, which imparted a frisson of additional excitement to their relationship. There was excitement enough as both were new to romance and to the tentative sexual exploration that went with it.

Lubec had only 682 households and 356 families. Some of Robin and

Adam's friends told other friends or a parent about their relationship and it did not take long for it to become widely known. Even John Cross of the *Quoddy Times*, heard about it and saw trouble coming. He had done a story about their school class and its charity drive, had interviewed them both in connection with it, and thought them nice kids.

*

Ron got the word from one of his fellow Trump supporters. There were five of them having a beer at the end of the workday. The conversation was jovial, and Ron asked his friend about his community service. He shrugged his shoulders. "It's not bad at all. I'm driving some elderly people to medical and other appointments, and most of them are nice folks. I do have to wear a mask, which I don't like."

"Did you drive anybody to see Dr. Zarchy?" one of them asked, provoking laughter.

"Not yet. But I don't go inside. I just drop people off."

"I hear his son goes inside," another quipped.

Ron looked at him with raised eyebrows.

"Don't you know? He's dating your daughter."

"He's what?"

"Adam is stepping out with Robin."

"You're putting me on."

"No, I'm not. It's the talk of the town."

Ron reached for his beer can and sucked in a good mouthful. It was not a good idea as the carbonation tickled his nasal passage. "I can't believe she would betray me like this."

One of the other friends spoke up. "He's a nice lad. A summer back we were both fishing off the pier and had a good chat. He seemed a down-to-earth fellow."

"My daughter is a grade ahead and she likes him too."

"No daughter of mine is going out with that SOB's son. I bet he's laughing his head off about it."

Ron decided to go home in lieu of having a second beer. He would get to the bottom of the matter sooner rather than later.

*

The Zarchys also learned second-hand about their daughter's boyfriend. Mary Zarchy was an engineer who specialized in the miniaturization of instruments, many of them used in space or underwater exploration, but now also in medicine. She had worked for a big company in one of their labs, but she and her husband, both Down Easters by origin, decided they would prefer to raise their children in Maine than southern California. They moved to Lubec where Alex took over the practice of an elderly internist. Mary freelanced. She did not really need a lab for her work, although she missed the social interactions with her colleagues. She worked primarily on a computer, and thanks to the Internet had constant contact with people who assembled and tested what she had designed.

She was on-line that afternoon chatting with members of a team in Texas who were struggling to fabricate one of her instruments. The problem was mechanical; they could not program their machines to perform one of the operations critical to assembly. With knowledge of the problem, they hoped, she might figure out some way to design around it. With the business out of the way they exchanged a few pleasantries. One of them asked if her son's name was Adam, and she said yes.

"My son Tyrone spends too much time surfing the web. I don't know how or why, but yesterday he came across a posting from Quoddy Head. He knows that I work long-distance with someone from Lubec. Some time back he googled the town to see where it was and discovered Quoddy Head State Park. He loves the name Quoddy and thinks it really exotic. So he was drawn to a post that had the name of the Park and showed a partially undressed couple lying in the grass. Some snoop with a telephoto lens was having a field day. Their names were given below the photos and Tyrone remembered that my contact in Lubec is a woman named Zarchy."

"I don't know what to say."

"Do you want me to send you the URL?"

"No, definitely not. I respect my son's privacy, even if other people don't."

After finishing her Zoom meeting, Mary went for her almost daily run. It was late summer but breezy and chilly, so she donned a nylon top. She had several running routes and chose the one with the smoothest surface so she would not constantly have to look at her feet. She wanted to minimize distractions so she could think. She remembered her own adolescence, her first crush on a boy, and the first time she kissed one. It was in a clearing behind her bunk at summer camp. The memory brought a smile to her face even though she was jogging at a good clip. "thank god," she thought, "there was no Internet in those days and nobody – to her knowledge – photographed her. I would have been mortified," she thought. "What the world has come to."

Mary decided not to share her knowledge with John or to say a word to Adam. He was responsible and she could only hope they had not gone too far on the sexual front as they were both so young. The topic nevertheless came up because Alex had heard about the relationship from one of his nurses. He told Mary, who confessed that she too had learned about, but only this morning. They decided they should have a tête-à-tête with Adam during dinner since he was the talk of the town.

Adam was surprised that both his parents had been told about his relationship, to which he readily admitted.

"Robin is a lovely girl and we've known each other all our lives."

"We've met her," Mary said, "although we certainly don't know her well."

"We're not getting married, mom."

"I didn't think you were. We bring it up because everyone knows about it, talks about, and tweets about it." Mary, and then Alex, told Adam how they heard about his romance."

"Somebody's posted pictures of us?"

"It seems so."

"Have you seen them."

"Absolutely not. You're entitled to a private life."

"You're a saint, mom."

"Not really, but I try to be a good mother."

"What are Robin's politics like?" Alex asked.

"I have no idea. We've never discussed it."

"Never talked politics?" her father said.

"That's right. Everybody else in school does, almost incessantly. I'm sick of it, and I imagine Robin is too."

"How could you not think about politics when our democracy is at risk?"

"That's just it. There's nothing I can do about it. I'm not even old enough to vote. Like you, I'm hoping Trump is defeated, but for now I've put it aside. I'm trying to live my life."

Alex reached out to touch the arm of his son. "I understand. I was a bit too aggressive."

"Not for the first time, dad."

"I'm sorry. May I ask you a question?"

"Depends on what it is."

"Fair enough. I assume Robin's parents also know about the two of you?"

"I don't know. We agreed to keep it secret. But if you have both heard about it it's likely her parents have to. I'm going to ask her."

"If they do," Alex said, "they won't be at all happy about it."

"Yes, I hear her dad is a loose cannon. Her mother is fearful of him and dares not contradict him. Robin says he struts about like a rooster."

"How does he treat her?" her mother asks.

"He doesn't abuse her, if that's what you are asking. Robin says he expects her to serve him, think like him, and do his bidding. I shouldn't really say this, but she is unhappy at home and can't wait to escape to university."

"I can imagine," his father said. "Have you ever been in their house."

"No way! The last thing I want to do is cause trouble. You and he aren't exactly bosom pals."

"The bastard threw a rock through our window and cut my tires!"

"Tell me about it."

*

The discussion in the Sweeny home went somewhat differently. Ron strode in and asked his wife where their daughter was. "Upstairs with a friend studying for a test."

"I want her down here now."

"Ron, sit down and let me get you a beer. Let the poor girl study for her biology test."

"I don't want a beer, I want her. Go get her."

Mrs. Sweeny turned around and slowly walked upstairs. Ron went into the kitchen and took a beer out of the fridge. He opened it, thought about grabbing a bag of chips to go with it, but resisted the temptation because he was putting on weight. He returned to the parlor as his wife was coming down the stairs.

"Where is she?" he asked.

"She says she'll be down when she finishes studying."

"I want her now."

"You'll just have to wait. Let her be."

Ron headed up the stairs to Robin's room. His wife could hear him rapping with some force on her closed door. A muffled conversation followed, there was a pause, and Ron came downstairs with both girls following him.

Robin's friend said goodbye to her mother and left the house.

Ron restrained himself until the door had shut and Robin's friend could be seen walking across the slate stone walk to her bike.

"You have some explaining to do," he said.

Robin had remained standing with fists clenched at her side. "You're the one who needs to do that. What's gotten into you? You drag me away from my studies and embarrass me in front of a friend?"

"You've done much worse than embarrass me."

"What have I done?"

"What have you done? You know damn well what you've done!"

"I don't know what you're talking about."

"You damn well do!" Ron realized he was gripping his beer can and placed it on the table. You're going out with Adam Zarchy. For all I know you're spreading your legs for him."

"Ron," his wife said. "That's no way to talk to your daughter."

"You keep out of this, you hear me?"

"You're disgusting," Robin said.

Ron smacked her in the face.

Robin was stunned. He had never hit her before. Her mother gasped. Robin ran upstairs and disappeared into her room.

"Now you've done it," Ron's wife said. "It wasn't enough to tear down signs and slash tires. You have to hit your daughter too." Ron sunk into his chair and reached for his beer. They sat there in uncompanionable silence.

A few minutes later Robin could be heard coming down the stairs. Both parents looked in her direction. She had changed into jeans and was wearing a parka and over that, a backpack.

"Where are you going?" her mother asked.

"Far away from here!"

"You can't do that," her father said.

Robin looked at her mother as he headed for the door. "I'll call."

Her parents were stunned and watched as Robin rode off on her bike.

Ron was the first to speak. "If she's going to his house, I'll kill her."

*

Robin biked to her study chum and asked if she could spend the night.

"What happened?" Anna asked.

"I don't want to go into it now, but I can't return home."

"Is it your father?"

"Yes." Robin stared into space.

Anna was sensitive enough not to pry, thought for a moment, and then said: "My mom is due home soon. Let's go upstairs and finish studying. I'll ask her if you can stay the night. She's almost certain to agree."

Adam and Robin texted each other regularly and she had three texts from him waiting on her phone. She couldn't face telling him what had happened so sent a quick message that she was studying for their biology test and would see him at school tomorrow.

Anna's mother returned and agreed that she could spend the night if it was all right with her parents. Robin did not want to lie and gambled that her mother would answer the phone when she called. She guessed right and Robin told her that she would be spending the night at Anna's. Her mother was relieved that she had not left town or done anything foolish and immediately agreed.

*

The following morning Anna's mom made them both breakfast and sandwiches to take to school for lunch. She was impressed by Robin's clearing of the table and offer to help with the dishes. "No worries," she said. "Off to school the two of you, and good luck on the test."

Robin saw Adam briefly when she and Anna walked into home room. He was talking to friends, and she nodded at him. They went to biology class, where she saw him again, this time a couple of rows away in his assigned seat. They smiled at each other again as the teacher passed out the test. Robin did her best to concentrate on it and once she got into it found it a form of therapy. For the first time since her father had slapped her, she was able to put him out of her mind and concentrate on something else.

The test went quickly but the rest of the school day dragged on. She ate lunch with the usual group of friends, but not with Adam who was off running an errand. The afternoon went on forever, but she and Adam exchanged furtive texts.

"Need to c u 😊."

"ILY (I love you) 😊🖤

"I'm in 😔."

"???"

"Meet at 3? 🖤😔🚲to QH?"

"TTYL (talk to you later)

FTW (best left untranslated)

*

Robin and Adam met at the bike rack and pedaled off together in the direction of Quoddy Head. As their relationship was public knowledge there was no longer any need for subterfuge. It was a nice day and the warmth of the sun and the sea breeze felt good. Adam slowed down to turn into the beach, but Robin shouted at him and waved him off. She took the lead and went further out until she came to an area that looked completely deserted. She motioned him to follow her on to a sandy track. It was hard biking and after about ten feet she dismounted, as did Adam. Robin ignored his question as to where they were going and pressed ahead until they reached a cliff. They laid the bikes on the sea grass, and she raised her fingers to her lips when he began to speak. Adam said nothing but followed her to the edge of the cliff, where he saw there was an easy descent to a small plateau protected by rock face on two sides and providing an impressive outlook on the bay. Once on the plateau Robin turned and pressed herself against him. Adam stroked her hair and they kissed.

Breaking off the embrace and stepping back, Robin said: "We need to talk."

"What's up? I hope you're still happy with me?" Adam said in an anxious voice.

Robin embraced him again. "Of course, I am. It has nothing to do with us. Well, actually, it has everything to do with us."

Adam was now completely befuddled. Robin saw the expression on his and laughed. "Come give me another kiss and I will tell all."

Adam needed no further encouragement, put his arms around her, and drew her face to his.

Suitably reassured, Adam allowed Robin to lead him to the edge of the plateau where they sat down next to each other, legs dangling over a ledge with another plateau about four feet below them. There were puffins nesting on a rocky outcrop in the bay, and some of the little ones looked like they were about to fledge. There were also Herring Gulls circling the cliff, and they made quite a racket. The scene was nevertheless tranquil and created the much-needed distance from Lubec.

"The cat is out of the bag," Robin said. "Everybody knows about us, including my parents."

"Yeah, mine too."

"How did they respond?"

"Better than I supposed. They took it in the stride. My mom says that there are photos on-line of us necking. That shook me up. I don't how it happened or who did it, or why they posted it. Mom was angry about the photos, not about us lying in the grass. She said we have a right to privacy and refused to look at the pictures."

"Wow! That's really nice of her. What about your dad? Was he upset when he found out who I am?"

"Not really. He did ask me about your politics and I told him we never talk politics."

"I hear enough of it at home."

"Does your father proselytize you?"

"And my mom. He wants us to become Trump supporters. He even bought be a MAGA hat."

"Are you?"

Robin prodded him gently in his belly with her fist.

"I'm sorry."

"It's OK. Trump is disgusting and so is my father. Politics turns me off. And you?"

"Dad keeps saying that democracy is at risk and I keep telling him there is nothing I can do about it."

"So who took pictures of us?"

"I don't have a clue," Adam confessed. "The only people I see here with cameras are families on the beach or bird watchers. Some of them have big telephoto lenses and tripods."

"You think it was some dirty old man who got bored with his birds?"

"I don't know. I just hope it wasn't someone from school who followed us out here, took the pictures, and showed them to all our friends."

"It could be. They've all seen them on-line, I'm sure. I bet some of our teachers have too. I haven't seen them, so I don't know what they show. You had your top off so . . . ."

"Yech," Robin exclaimed. "It's disgusting. Why would old people be interested in sex? Anyway, that's not our problem. Although, it is why I brought you here. It's a very private space. We're invisible to anything but a drone."

Adam did a quick recce of the sky. Robin laughed. She pulled up her shirt exposing her brassiere and rotated in both directions. "It's a free show, you creeps," she shouted. In a quieter voice she said to Adam: "I hope my tiny boobs don't disappoint."

"I love your tiny tits," he said.

"How did your parents respond?"

"That's what I need to talk to you about." Robin described her encounter with her father and her storming out of her parents' house. She did not want to return but had nowhere to go. Looking across at the rock with the puffins, she said: "I'm just the opposite of those fledglings. They're capable of flying off on their own but reluctant to leave home. Their parents will ultimately persuade them to go. I'm desperate to leave, have no wings, and parents who want to keep me in their spoiled nest."

"I could speak to my parents. Maybe you could move in with us?"

"That'll never work, even if they agree. My father will be all over them – and me, if he catches me on the street."

"I see your point. What do you suggest?"

"Much as I'd like too, we can't just run off. We need to finish school to have a life, and we have to do that here in Lubec."

"Could you live with one of your friends' families? It wouldn't be so in the face of your father."

"I thought of that. He'll kidnap me and I suspect the law will be on his side as I am a minor."

"A minor with a major problem."

"So what are we going to do about it?"

"I have a plan."

*

Ron was still seething. Robin had walked out of his house. His wife said nothing but it was clear that she took her side. He wondered if all of this had not been planned. "Maybe Zarchy had pushed his son into dating Robin and then the two of them turned her against him. It was unnatural for a daughter to reject her father. It's the kind of thing communist-leaning Democrats would do. They were already teaching school kids to become fags and socialists. So why not go a step further and plot against their fathers? Nazis and communists taught children to spy on their parents. The Democrats were taking this from their playbook. And they accused the right of conspiracies!"

Ron knew that Robin had spent the night at the home of a school friend. Clever too, he thought. The Zarchys probably arranged this all in advance. He wondered if their son had spent the night there too? By now he had heard about and checked out the photos that had been posted on-line. You couldn't see much but it was clear that his daughter had taken off her shirt and that Adam was lying on top of her. "What had happened to his little girl? She used to adore him. They had good times together fishing and on his snowmobile. When she played soccer, he had gone as many games as he could and cheered for her and her team. Life had been good but now his family was falling apart. Maybe he had been a little harsh and should not have hit her."

Ron's anger morphed into self-pity and then he went into a deep funk. He tried calling Robin's cell, but she did not answer. He tried again ten minutes later and left a brief message: "I love you. Please call."

Ron drove into town. The general store had good fresh pastries and he knew exactly what kind Robin liked the best. His wife liked them too so he would buy some and hope that life might return to normal. He had stopped patronizing the general store but decided to make an exception for the pastries. When he walked in – wearing a mask -- Sam was signing a receipt for the milk delivery man. He did not see Adam Zarchy in the far corner holding a metal shopping basket. The two men arrived at the pastry counter at almost the same moment. Adam was first and waited for Sam to appear. In the old days there were tongs customers could use to help themselves. The pandemic had done away with self-service everywhere. Sam appeared and said good morning to both men. They acknowledged his greeting but studiously ignored each other.

"Adam, what would you like?" Sam said.

"Three pieces of cheese danish, thanks."

Ron started to say something but stopped himself. His face turned red and he began shaking.

"Are you alright?" Sam asked.

Alex then turned around to have a look. "You really look distressed. Perhaps you should sit down for a moment. Sam, can you bring a chair?"

Ron didn't know what to do. His heart was racing, he was feeling weak all of a sudden, and he could feel the arteries above his cheekbones throbbing.

"I'm all right," he finally said. "Dr. Zarchy . . . he . . . he threw me for a loop."

"Do you hate me that much?

"No, it's the pastries"

"The pastries?"

"Yes, you bought the ones I wanted and there aren't any left. They're my wife's favorites and my daughter's too. I was bringing them home as a special treat."

"Not a problem," said Alex. "Sam, would you mind giving Ron the bag."

Sam hand the bag with the pastries inside over the counter to Ron, who paused before reaching out for them."

"Are you sure?" he said to Alex.

"Yes, of course. Have a nice brunch with your family."

Ron took his wallet out to pay.

Alex raised his hand. "Be my guest. Next time is your treat."

Ron thanked him and walked slowly to the door.

After he had left, Sam raised his head up and down, bit his lower lip to signal "well done."

"I was worried about him," Sam said. "I thought he was having a heart attack."

"Something's not right," Alex agreed. "I was thinking my appearance had provoked it and was getting ready to catch him if he fell."

"You did a good deed."

"Maybe. I hope they have a nice brunch and that our relationship improves.

Sam nodded in agreement.

"You won't tell anybody about this?" Alex said. "I don't want to embarrass him."

""Not a word. I promise."

*

Robin asked her friend if she could stay another night and called her mother at work to get her permission. They came up with a good story for why she needed a second night away from home. When Robin's phone rang and she saw it was her father she did not answer. The call she was waiting for did not arrive until a good hour later. It was from a friend on Campobello Island, where she was planning temporary refuge. It was in another country and would make it that much more difficult for her father to force her to come home.

Adam and Robin played hooky the next morning to put their plan into effect. It was inspired by *Romeo and Juliet*. Robin had also begun to think of herself as Juliet and had fantasies of punishing her family by taking a sleeping potion. Her family – her father, anyway – qualified as a Capulet. But Adam's family were not exactly Montagues. They did not punish him for dating Robin and, to the best of her knowledge, had never uttered a negative word about her. They fit only in the sense that they were horrified by her father and his associates. There was a real feud between the families; each associated with a different political party and those parties were at war, almost in a literal sense. Robin suggested that Adam might be able to get his hands on a suitable drug as his father was a doctor and surely had something lying around the house. Adam disabused her of the notion. Her father's drugs were under lock and key in his office and at the hospital. He would never steal anything from him even if he could, and he didn't want her taking something that might do real damage.

Adam thought *Prospero and Caliban* might be a better fit. Leonato is completely controlling of his daughter Hero. He nevertheless welcomes the advances of the elderly suitor Don Pedro. When rumor is spread that Hero is no longer pure – by word of mouth rather than on the Internet -- he is outraged that his daughter is unchaste and furious that people are talking negatively about his child. Robin agreed that her father was like Leonato but had not encouraged any suitor. He wanted to keep her virginal and his "little girl."

"My father also resembles King Lear," she said. He is full of questionable expressions of fatherly love. Lear thinks he is in command, but his daughters really rule the kingdom. Dad acts like a king, but it's my mother who holds the house together. He's never set tests for me or played me off against my mother. But I can certainly see him descending into madness – and like Lear, the catalyst would be his daughter's rebellion."

"How'd you do on the bio test?" Adam asked.

 "Why for god's sake are you asking me about that now?"

"I was thinking you would have absolutely aced an English test."

Robin chuckled.

"If you really wanted to drive your father mad you would volunteer to work on Biden's election campaign."

"That might do it, but I don't want to make him crazy. I want to make him sane.

"You don't want him to walk into the sea?"

"No, I want the sea to cultivate his sense of humility. That's what it did for Lear."

"I packed all my gear," Adam said," but I confess to second thoughts about our plan. My parents will have a fit until I reappear safely and god knows how yours will react. Something like this could produce the opposite of what we intend."

"That's occurred to me too but I can't think of another way out. I'm willing to accept the risk. What about you?"

"Yes, I love you and will go along even if it's against my better judgment." Adam refrained from telling Robin that he had a quiet chat with his parents and told them that they might hear that something terrible had happened but it wouldn't have, he would be all right, and they shouldn't worry. They were upset and wanted to know what was going on, but he wouldn't tell them.

"OK then, are we ready?" Robin asked.

"Give me a kiss first," Adam demanded.

Robin was happy to oblige. They then walked together to their bikes. As Robin was mounting hers her phone rang. "I'm not answering it," she said.

"Just have a look to see who it is."

Robin had a quick peek. "It's my mother." Robin held the cell phone and listened to it sound.

"Why not answer it? It won't keep us from our plan."

Robin swiped the screen and held the phone to her ear. She listened for a bit and then said: "Yes, mom, I'm OK." Then after another pause: "Don't worry about the school. It's the least of our problems. Anyway, I got the second highest grade in the biology test." She waited for her mother to finish speaking and said "let me think about it, mom. I'll call you back."

"What did she say?"

'She was worried about me, and so is my father."

"He has a strange way of showing his affection."

"Mom says he feels terrible about having hit me, wants to apologize, and has invited us both to brunch. He apparently went to the General Store – despite his oath never to set foot in it again – to buy my favorite pastry."

"What do you want to do?"

"I don't know. Our crazy venture had the goal of provoking the kind of about-face my father seems to have made."

"I feel much relieved."

"You don't think we should go through with it?"

"From what you said it sounds unnecessary. And what kind of pastry did you say he bought?"

Robin couldn't reach his ribs to poke so flipped him the bird.

"Cheese danish, if you must know."

"Yummy."

"I interpret that to mean that I – rather we – should accept."

"Am I really invited?"

Robin nodded.

"That's an invitation I don't think we can refuse."

Robin found her mom's number in her contact list and pressed call.

*

Robin and Adam biked back into town to Robin's house. Her parents were waiting on the steps and gave Robin a big hug. Her mother pushed back a few tears. Both parents introduced themselves to Adam, who shook Ron's hand when he offered it.

"It's a nice day," Robin's mother Sylvia said ."What if we had our brunch on the patio table in the garden? They readily agreed and Sylvia went inside to fetch coffee for everyone.

Ron took Robin's hand and led the way to the patio. He asked Adam if he could have a few minutes alone with his daughter. Adam said he would have a walk around the block.

"I am really very sorry," Ron said to Robin. "I promise to act differently in the future. I love you very much." Ron reached out to embrace his daughter and she allowed him to do so.

"I love you too, dad. But you've been a different person of late."

"I'll return to my old self, I promise."

"I really hope so."

"I still feel strongly about Trump and defending our basic freedoms, but I shouldn't impose my opinions on you and your mom."

"What about Adam?"

"I hope he's a nice lad. I had a strange encounter with his father this morning."

"Another fight!"

"We exchanged words in the General Store this morning."

"You had another rift with him?"

"No, no, pleasant words."

Robin paused to process this revelation.

Ron explained what had happened and also how he suddenly felt faint and short of breath when he thought he was too late to purchase the pastries. "I so wanted to bring them home to you and Sylvia."

"How nice of Dr. Zarchy. His son is cut from the same cloth. I'm hoping you grow to like him."

"I will try to do that. Tell me, the two of you . . ."

Seeing what was coming, Robin hastened to cut him off. "Dad, let's not go there."

Sylvia came out with coffee, milk, and cups on a tray. "Let me just go back and get the pastries."

"No, you stay here and talk to Robin. I'll fetch them", said Ron.

Ron took the now empty tray inside and Adam reappeared.

Sylvia served coffee and Adam took a seat next to Robin.

Ron returned with three pastries on a plate on the tray.

"I'll forego one," Sylvia said. "Ron didn't know there would be four of us."

"No, please have one," said Ron. "I'm going to pass. I noticed last night that I've lost my taste for food."

'Lost your taste," Sylvia said in an alarmed voice. "You eat like a horse. Are you well?"

"I had no energy this morning, but appetite is not my problem. I've lost my sense of taste."

"That's a sign of COVID," Sylvia proclaimed. "Are you short of breath?"

"A little and I think it's getting worse."

"Let's get you to the doctor," she announced.

A NIGHT AT THE OPERA

The woodwinds sounded a minor chord as Oedipus fell to his knees. Blind, overcome by pain and grief, he remained motionless several bars after the sound of the woodwinds died away. Slowly and unsteadily Oedipus then rose and stared with unseeing eyes at the audience. Two violins quietly began the famous fugue that ends Act III. When the cellos introduced the second voice, Oedipus groped his way towards the far right of the dimly lit stage and made his final exit.

The applause began before the last notes of the fugue had sounded. Erika rose from her seat, propelled by her enthusiasm for the performance, and through the act of clapping sought release from the tension of the last act. Hans, in the seat alongside, had been deeply moved too but could not bring himself to express his feelings so openly. He envied Erika her ability to do so. Three curtain calls later, her tension spent, Erika turned to Hans who took her hand and guided her gently through the crowd toward the exit.

The night was brisk but not uncomfortable, and the couple, still holding hands, walked down the *Unter den Linden* in the direction of the *Brandenburger Tor*. They stopped for a traffic light and Erika broke the silence between them.

"Wasn't I right?"

"It was stunning," Hans agreed. I'm glad we went."

"What did you think of Sussmann?"

The pedestrian signal turned green, and Hans led Erika into the intersection. He waited to answer her question until they were safely across the street. "He's the perfect Mozartian hero. He has a powerful but controlled voice. I thought he made the transition from fiery youth to mature statesman very convincingly."

Erika nodded. "As I see it, *Oedipus* is about the parallel conflicts between man's desire to assert free will against the fate he fears will determine his destiny. Oedipus unwittingly violates a taboo and punishes himself for this transgression. I like the way Mozart has the baritone sing *stonato* to convey Oedipus' internal conflict, and Sussmann does it as well as anybody I've heard."

"I sing off tune all the time, *schatz*."

Not deliberately!"

Hans gave her hand a squeeze.

The couple strolled along the perimeter of the *Tiergarten*. At Hans' suggestion, they entered a cafe and took a table within reach of the heat of the large, open-hearth fire burning seasoned oak from one of the many forests surrounding the city. A waiter appeared and wrote down their orders: cappuccino for Erika, a *pils* for Hans.

Erika reached into her pursue, pulled out a pack of cigarettes, put one in her mouth and lit it with a small, gold lighter. Using both hands, she pushed her long blond hair back from her angular face. Hans recognized the gesture as a warning sign that Erika had something serious on her mind. He was nevertheless surprised when she leaned forward to ask what the world would have been like if Mozart had died a young man.

"What would the world be like?" Hans repeated her question.

"Yes. Would life be any different like today? Would Mozart's premature death have changed things in any way? Would we be sitting here having a drink?"

"I've never given it any thought. I certainly hope I'd still be sitting here with you."

"I hope so too." Erika reached across to give his arm a squeeze.

"If Mozart had died young. . . . " Hans paused to consider the problem. "Well, we wouldn't have any of his mature works. There would be no *Oedipus*, no *Werther* and no late piano and violin sonatas or symphonies, including my favorite, fifty-seven."

"True enough, but that's not what I had in mind. I was thinking about the broader artistic and political ramifications."

"I can see another one of your zany ideas is about to sally forth."

"You're just a stick in the mud, Hans. Suppose Mozart had been run over by a carriage when he was your age, thirty-five. His last opera would have been *La Clemenza di Tito*, a wonderful score to be sure, but an old-fashioned opera *seria*, and a far cry from his mature, tragic works." Erika took a drag on her cigarette, and Hans lifted his mug his beer to his mouth. He waited for Erika to continue, as he knew she would.

"The post-classical movement would have been stillborn. Da Ponte, who wrote the libretti for *Cosi fan Tutte*, *Marriage of Figaro* and *Don Giovanni*, had to flee Vienna after some count caught him in bed with his wife. Mozart did not find an equally gifted collaborator until he teamed up with Neuman in 1805. That's when he really began to explore the meaning of social justice and what kind of society would allow man to reconcile competing needs. *Oedipus*, *Orestes*, and *Luisa Miller* are vehicles for this analysis. Each opera examines some aspect of the problem in a more complex way, intellectually and artistically."

"Mozart wasn't alone in addressing these themes."

"That's my point, Hans. In the early nineteenth century, music was the most *avant garde* of the art forms. Mozart's mature compositions established a philosophical framework not only for music, but for literature and art, and even politics. Schubert and Mendelssohn's music, Schiller and Shelley's poetry, carried on and developed the post-classical tradition. Without Mozart, Romanticism would have dominated the artistic life of Europe and the political consequences would have been profound and frightening."

"Come on, Erika. I know you despise Romanticism, but that's an extraordinary allegation."

"Bear with me, Hans. Romanticism represents the untrammeled expression of individualism. Man ruled by his emotions, egoistic, self-indulgent, and unconcerned with the consequences of his actions for others. Beethoven, Byron, Siegfried -- all the romantic heroes, real and fictional, are like this. Political leaders who were influenced by romantic ideals would have made conflict a virtue, compromise suspect, and passion in public life something to reward rather than constrain, and this at a time when rapid economic development and social change were creating great political strains. What if Romanticism had become the crucible for strong nationalist movements whose leaders were not above using violence to achieve their goals? It would have been very difficult, maybe impossible, to accommodate the various struggles for reform or independence that developed in the last century."

"Your imagination never ceases to amaze me. But I don't buy your argument. All those mass movements were attempts by disenfranchised classes to gain a share of political and economic power. The Repeal Movement in Ireland was the prototype. In the 1840's, Daniel O'Connell raised the prospect of political separation to compel the British to restore an Irish parliament with substantial autonomy from London. Other oppressed groups followed suit and met with varying degrees of success. The most serious confrontation was in the Habsburg Empire where the leadership's rigidity, suppression of dissent and the late development of a middle class threatened to unleash chaos. Fortunately, cooler heads prevailed. Under the aegis of Germany, France and Britain, a federal solution was worked out in 1878. Admittedly, it provoked a backlash by segments of the Empire's German and Hungarian communities, who until then had all but monopolized political and economic power."

"Don't minimize our country's problems, Hans. Remember the *Vaterlandspartei* in the second half of the century mobilized support from groups who had been marginalized by the industrial revolution. Beckstein, its leader until the great scandal, blamed the Jews for all of Germany's problems. He drew substantial support from the lower, middle and artisan classes and disaffected intellectuals. As I recall, the *Vaterlandspartei* captured close to twenty percent in the 1894 elections; they were helped, of course, by the economic crisis. During the Great Depression we had a similar if less successful movement, led by that crazy Austrian, Hitler."

"He was a real flake." Hans raised his right arm in imitation of Hitler's signature salute.

"Ask yourself Hans why Beckstein and Hitler were flashes in the pan."

"That's pretty obvious. The 1849 constitution created the framework for a stable, decentralized, and democratic Germany. All the German states except for Austria sooner or later joined the confederation. Prussia, the most powerful and least democratic, was ultimately compelled to reform its electoral system. After that, it was only a matter of time before political power passed from the *Junkers* to the liberal industrialists. The more serious problem was labor unrest in northern Germany, Silesia, and the Rhineland. But once again, compromises were worked out, difficult as they were, and social democracy moderated its demands. German corporatism became the model for most of the rest of Europe. Because our political system was widely accepted as legitimate, neither Beckstein nor Hitler made much headway, even in times of economic crisis and widespread unemployment."

"You get honors in history, Hans. Now let me return to my counterfactual. Suppose in the absence of post-classicism, Romanticism had come to dominate the artistic and political culture of the nineteenth century? Movements for reform would almost certainly have been movements for independence, and their leaders would not have sought independence as a means to an end but as an end in itself."

"I don't follow you?"

Erika brushed the hair back from around her cheeks and lit another cigarette. "In the latter half of the nineteenth century, many political movements demanded independence to extract political and economic concessions from governments. The threat usually worked, and the idea of independence, not very practical in most cases, was shelved. In Quebec, they still play this game. A unified Italy made sense, and Vienna accepted the inevitable, but think what would have happened if the Habsburg Empire had been divided into a half-dozen so-called national states. None of these entities would have been viable economically. True 'national' states would have been impossible in practice because the various language communities are so geographically intermingled throughout the region. Hungarians and Rumanians would have laid claim to Transylvania, Czechs and Germans to Bohemia, Poles and Germans to Silesia, Italians and Germans to Tirol, Slovenes, Croats and Italians to Istria – *und so weiter*. The Habsburg successor states would have fragmented into still small units and fought one another over disputed territories. I shudder to think of the consequences, especially in the Balkans."

"It's a ridiculous situation to contemplate, I admit. But you haven't answered my question."

"Sorry about the digression, *Schatz*. Have you ever read Herder?"

"We discussed him in *Gymnasium*, but I don't remember much. Some mystical nonsense about a nation being the organic expression of the soul of a people."

"That's the gist of it. The traditional concept of a nation included all of the inhabitants of a political unit organized in several estates. For Herder, a nation was a group of people who belonged to a specific language or cultural community, regardless of where they resided. They had a right -- a duty actually -- to organize themselves politically in a 'nation state.' Some of Herder's successors carried his dangerous notion a step further by arguing that nations competed in a Darwinian world in which only the fittest would survive. To be one of history's winners, a nation had to become strong and carve out a niche for itself at the expense of its neighbors and competitors. Imagine a Europe of nation states with foreign policies based on the narrowest calculations of self-interest!"

"It would have been grim."

"That's putting it mildly! Even in Western Europe, so-called nation states would have included substantial minorities who might have faced all kinds of discrimination. In Germany, the obvious target was the Jews. From the time of the crusades, they were the scapegoat for anything that went wrong. Beckstein and Hitler tried with only limited success to arouse hatred of Jews, but they might have succeeded in a different Germany."

"Now you're really getting carried away. France may have been the first country to tear down its ghettos, but Germany went much further than any of its neighbors in eradicating age-old prejudices. By the end of the nineteenth century Jews, their religious practices aside, were indistinguishable from other citizens. Every schoolchild learns about the contributions they made to the scientific, cultural, and economic life of our country. They even gave us our sense of humor. We Germans are an enlightened and tolerant people. This is why Beckstein and Hitler's hate-mongering fell on largely deaf ears."

"Don't be so smug! It didn't have to be that way. In the absence of post-classicism, the twentieth century could have turned out very differently. Germany, France, and Britain, the three great democracies, were an axis of stability in a Europe reeling from the consequences of rapid industrialization. Without a common liberal framework to unite them, the great powers could have been at each other's throats as they had always been in the past. Look at Asia. Modernization in the absence of a common political culture, mutual economic dependence, and accepted mechanisms for resolving international disputes led to a series of destructive wars. Romantic nationalism would have undermined the basis for international collaboration in Europe at the same time it would have encouraged more aggressive postures by the great powers. If Russia, Austria-Hungary, and maybe even Germany, had adopted expansionist foreign policies to cope with their domestic problems, a major European war would have been hard to avoid. Suppose Germany and Austria-Hungary had lost such a war. Afterwards, some nut like Hitler, who attributed the defeat to a Jewish-socialist conspiracy, might well have found a receptive audience."

"That's over the top!"

"Why?"

"Since the Enlightenment, Europe has witnessed the steady advance of reason and progress. Education, science, and economic development have banished ignorance, superstition, and poverty to the remotest corners of the continent. These developments have deep, structural causes. They are not dependent on particular individuals. It's very unlikely that the premature death of any artist could have profound consequences for the cultural development of an entire civilization. And even if it did, the triumph of one mode of artistic expression over another could never have led to the kind of political consequences you describe. After a certain point, the development of a peaceful and prosperous Europe was all but inevitable."

"You're blinded by the hindsight bias."

"The what?"

"Did you ever read any psychology at university?"

"You must be kidding. Architecture students with time to read? But everybody knows about the cognitive revolution. Even *Leute von heute* had a story about Tversky and Kahneman and their institute in Vienna."

"*Leute von heute*? I didn't know you read such trash, Hans?"

"It was in my dentist's office."

"Did the article say anything about the research of Baruch Fischoff? He's one of Tversky and Kahneman's Polish colleagues?"

"I don't think so."

"Fischoff discovered the hindsight bias. He found that once an event occurs, people upgrade their prior estimate of its probability. They see the outcome as almost inevitable and become correspondingly insensitive to the role of contingency. The hindsight bias is one of the most ubiquitous and best documented of all cognitive biases."

"And you think I've fallen victim to it!"

"I do, *Schatz*.

"Well, I think you've gone too far in the other direction. If small changes in the world can have such large effects, then almost anything is possible. One more hit of caffeine and you'll tell me how different European history would have been if Emperor Franz Josef had lived to be an old man and his nephew Franz Ferdinand had never ascended to the throne. I can see the argument now. No Franz Ferdinand, no reforms, acute nationality problems in Austria-Hungary, and there's your European war."

"Who's getting carried away now!"

Review of Manuscript 98-248

The story examines a counterfactual world in which Wolfgang Amadeus Mozart died at the age of thirty-six. As a result, Europe became increasingly unstable and fought two destructive wars in the twentieth century. At the end of the first war, Austria-Hungary fragmented into a half-dozen unstable, independent states. Germany, the other big loser, also had to cede territory. A more fanatic version of Beckstein came to power, persecuted Germany's Jews, and started a second, unsuccessful war to regain Germany's lost territories.

The story is imaginative and reasonably well-written, and the two protagonists, an opera-loving couple, are engaging characters. All the action is in the first paragraph that describes the final scene of *Oedipus*. After the opera, Hans and Erika retire to a café where Erika poses the

Mozart counterfactual and describes its political implications to a sensibly dubious Hans.

The counterfactual is unconvincing. I can best demonstrate why by unpacking its first several steps. The antecedent, Mozart's premature death in 1791, is an acceptable minimal rewrite of history because thirty-five was close to the normal life expectancy in the era before modern medicine. Step two, in which the author contends that post-classicism never appeared, is highly problematic. Artistic styles capture or crystallize a society's mood. It is possible -- I think likely -- that some other composer, artist or writer, or combination of them, would have developed post-classicism in the absence of Mozart. Artistic movements, like other human innovations, arise when the time is ripe. Physics offers a good example. At least a score of scientists struggled to understand the deeper meaning of the Michelson-Morley discovery that the speed of light in a vacuum was constant, regardless of its direction relative to the motion of the earth. If Poincaré and Lorentz had not come up with their theory of relativity, somebody else like Planck or Einstein almost certainly would have.

The most Mozart's premature death could have accomplished would have been to delay the emergence and ultimate triumph of post-classicism. At least some cultural historians of the period argue that Haydn, among others, was already moving in this direction, and might have developed post-classicism without the help of Mozart. If so, then cultural history would have been put "back on track" and the consequences of Mozart's death would have been dampened down rather quickly. Today's world would not be precisely the same; as Hans rightly observes, we would not enjoy *Oedipus* and other late Mozart works, but the world would be the same in its general political and cultural outlines.

Let us nevertheless assume that post-classicism never developed, and that Romanticism became the dominant cultural movement. The author insists (step three) that its triumph would have had profound consequences for European politics. Romanticism's celebration of imagination over reason and expression over argument would somehow have transformed moderate reform movements into extreme, even violent ones, that sought to break up the great multi-national states that spanned Europe from the Rhine to the Urals. On the face of it, it is far-fetched to attribute such consequential political changes to variation in artistic style.

The political evolution of Central and Eastern Europe was largely determined by economics. Industrialization and trade produced a large and prosperous bourgeoisie, an educated and better-off working class, and the widely recognized need for economies of scale. There were tensions between the aristocracy and the new, rising classes, and these tensions were a contributing cause of revolution in France. By the end of the nineteenth century the economic benefits of industrialization were apparent to nearly everyone and the transformation it wrought in the distribution of income and education compelled changes in the political structure. Even Erika, who makes the counterfactual case, recognizes that only economic and political chaos would have resulted from fragmentation of the Austro-Hungarian Empire. So did key political actors from all classes and language groups; it was the principal incentive for them, with Germany's assistance, to work out a more democratic and federal structure for the Empire. The Magyar aristocracy, the biggest losers from these reforms, ultimately recognized that they too had much to gain from a peaceful and prosperous Balkans. Enlightened self-interest motivated the political restructuring of Austria-Hungary. It had nothing to do with the music to which people listened or the novels they read.

Counterfactual antecedents are linked to their consequents by a series of steps. Each of these steps is a development that is supposed to follow from the antecedent, and all of the steps are necessary to produce the consequent. The Mozart counterfactual contains at least six steps linking its antecedent (Mozart's death at age thirty-six) to the hypothesized consequent (an aggressive German regime in the twentieth century). Because Mozart dies young, (1) post-classicism fails to develop; (2) Romanticism emerges as the dominant form of artistic expression; (3) reform movements in central Europe become nationalist; (4) Austria-Hungary and Germany go to war to cope with domestic and foreign threats; (5) they are defeated; and (6) in the aftermath, an anti-Semitic dictator hell-bent on a revisionist war comes to power in Germany. Each of these counterfactuals assume other counterfactuals (e.g. Romanticism becomes dominant because no other artist develops post-classicism, Austria-Hungary behaves aggressively in the Balkans because Germany encourages it to do so instead of pushing Austria to reach an accommodation with its various linguistic communities; the victors in the first war are short-sighted, and unlike their predecessors at the Congress of Vienna, dismember the losers and then stand aside and allow an obvious madman to come to power in Germany and bully its neighbors). The probability of the consequent is the product of the probabilities of every step. If we grant a probability of 0.5 for each step -- and that is generous --- the overall probability of the consequent is a mere .016.

There is admittedly something arbitrary about determining the number of steps in any counterfactual. Like a fractal -- think of an ever longer coastline each time a map of it is enlarged to show more indentations -- a counterfactual can usually be sub-divided into an almost infinite number of steps. As a general rule, the more steps a counterfactual requires the lower its probability. But the smaller the changes in history introduced by any counterfactual, the greater its likelihood. Conceivably, the overall probability of a counterfactual might not change significantly as we break it down into more and more steps.

There is nevertheless a difference, difficult as it may be to identify in practice, between the minimal requirements of a counterfactual (as I have tried to describe for the Mozart counterfactual) and the enabling requirements of each of these steps. Let me illustrate this with a counterfactual of my own. Marcel was injured in an accident while driving to work yesterday morning. I maintain this would not have happened if he had not listened to music instead of the news on the radio while eating his breakfast. Marcel took a different route to work because he heard the newscaster announce that the road he normally takes was bumper-to-bumper in traffic. My counterfactual has two fundamental steps: Marcel does not listen to the radio and therefore does not change his route. There are many enabling steps: Marcel cannot slip on the ice while walking to the car, his car must start, and he must adhere to his regular route even when he discovers the highway ramp is backed up. The first two conditions have high probabilities. The third does not. Marcel might have responded to the tie up by crossing town via an alternate route. But he would likely have reached his office without incident because he would have arrived at the intersection where the accident took place at a different time and would not have been hit by the truck that earlier had spun out of control. Adding these enabling steps does not significantly affect the probability of Marcel arriving safely at his office.

Despite the improbability of the Mozart counterfactual, many readers will still find it convincing. People respond positively to narratives and numerous psychological experiments indicate that a story becomes more credible the more detail it contains. This is because probability judgments are not attached to events but to descriptions of events (Tversky and Kahneman, 1983; Tversky and Koehler, 1994). In a recent experiment, Lebow and Tetlock (2000) showed that "counterfactual unpacking" leads foreign policy experts to increase their estimate of the probability of historical events. The more details they provided about possible, alternative outcomes to the 1962 Cuban Sugar crisis (triggered by the European Federation's decision to give trade preferences to Cuban sugar while imposing stiff tariffs on American marketed sugar) the more likely the experts considered these outcomes. Lebow and Tetlock made no attempt to manipulate the number of steps between antecedents and consequents, but there is no reason why experiments could not be designed to do this.

The laws of statistical inference suggest that the probability of most compound counterfactuals will be low, and almost all counterfactuals that hypothesize major changes in the course of history have multiple links between their antecedents and consequents. Does this mean that history is impervious to manipulation by counterfactual thought experimentation? No, only that the past cannot be changed to produce at will some specific world at any temporal distance. There may be many alternative worlds in which great powers fight a war in the early twentieth century, but we cannot know with confidence what counterfactuals could generate them, and even less, the specific characteristics of the alternative worlds these counterfactuals, or combination of them, would have. Because many alternative worlds are possible, the probability of producing any one of them is low. For the same reason it is all but impossible to predict the future. Imagine a group of scholars meeting in 1815 to consider the character of the world a hundred years hence. Any world they describe would depend on numerous intervening steps. From the vantage point of 1815 the world in which we live today had a vanishingly low probability.

When thinking about contingency it is useful to distinguish between specific worlds and general sets of worlds. A specific world, like our own, has many features, one of which is the absence of a great power war. More importantly for our purposes, it is the result of a particular pathway of history. Our world is one instantiation of the set of all possible worlds in which there was no European war. A world in which Mozart died a young man would be a different world but still, I believe, a member of this set. Any number of other counterfactuals might produce other members of this set. There is also a class of worlds in which the great powers did fight a war, and Lebow and Tetlock came up with some reasonable counterfactuals for producing such a world. None of their counterfactuals involve the arts, and some of them, I think require more than minimal rewrites of history. The probability of producing a counterfactual world in either set of worlds is much greater than that of producing a specific member of either set. This is because there are more paths that lead to worlds in the set than to any one specific world.

The course of human events is admittedly more malleable than a superficial examination of probability would suggest. It may nevertheless be governed by something akin to Heisenberg's principle of uncertainty. There is an inverse relationship between the magnitude of change we want to produce in the world and our ability to know if any counterfactual(s) will produce this intended change. This is also true for changes we introduce in the real world to produce desired future consequences. The more radical the change (counterfactual or real), the more steps between the antecedent and its consequents, and the greater the temporal remove of these consequents, the more unpredictable the outcome of the experiment.

For the sake of simplicity, I assigned a 0.5 probability to every step in Mozart counterfactual, but the probability of these steps will almost certainly vary. Some steps may be more likely than others. In a world in which "national movements" demanded independence, it would have been difficult to have reached a political accommodation in Austria-Hungary, and thus, the probability of international conflict in the Balkans would also have been high. But I consider highly improbable the prior step on which the political stasis of Austria-Hungary depends: the determining influence of culture on the goals of reform movements in Eastern Europe. If the probability of one or more steps of a counterfactual is low, as I contend they are in the Mozart story, the likelihood of the consequent will be close to zero. If we assign a 0.1 probability to this step, and retain the 0.5 for all the other steps, the overall probability of the consequent is an insignificant .0031. If we assign higher probabilities to this and other steps, say 0.75, the likelihood of the consequent rises to .178 -- still less than one in five. To raise the probability over 0.5, the average probability of each step has to be at least 0.9 (this gives a total probability of 0.53), and this is very unlikely. This simple thought experiment indicates that for multiple step counterfactuals the probability of a consequent is more sensitive to the probability of individual steps than it is to the number of steps; even one step with a low probability will reduce significantly the probability of the consequent. While chains are only as strong as their weakest links, multiple counterfactuals are weaker than their weakest links.

The second assumption I made in calculating probability is that every fork leads to a meaningfully different alternative world. A six-step counterfactual like the Mozart story would generate sixty-four alternative worlds -- assuming each step had two forks and each of these steps had two forks, and so on out to six steps. Many of the steps in this counterfactual could have multiple (more than two) forks. In the absence of Mozart, Romanticism might entirely, largely, or only partially dominate the cultural life of Europe -- or not at all if some other artist developed a version of post-classicism. The war Germany and Austria lost could have had multiple outcomes in terms of its human and territorial cost, and the particular mix of the two would surely have affected the probability of a dictator coming to power afterwards. A six-step counterfactual could generate more than sixty-four alternative worlds. These worlds would all be different in at least some respects, but many of them would probably be the same with regard to the attributes that concern us. This is because "second order" consequences would lead some, perhaps, many, of the forks back to a few real or alternative worlds.

Counterfactuals track a specific chain of historical developments arising from an antecedent. Second order consequences are developments outside this chain that might also follow on the antecedent and that could affect the probability of the hypothesized consequent. There is a prize-winning history of the Peloponnesian War that argues that Athens could have won a victory early on if somebody else other than Pericles had been in charge and had pursued a more aggressive strategy against Sparta. But it is also likely that without Pericles, the Athenian assembly would not have reversed itself and offered an alliance to Corcyra. Without this alliance, war would not have arisen, and the counterfactual would have been moot. If we do away with some individual or development, we may also create a "niche" that other individuals or organizations fill. Earlier I suggested that without Mozart, some other composer, perhaps Haydn, might have developed post-classicism and put cultural history back on track. Second-order consequences can also affect the significance of the consequent, even if it does occur. Suppose we invent minimal rewrites that reverse the outcome of the Battle of Poitiers in 732, allowing Muslim invaders to penetrate France. If Muslim kingdoms in northern Spain continued their internecine fighting, weakening their overall power and drive to expand beyond the Pyrenées, then the benefits of their military success at Poitiers might have been short-lived. Second order consequences would rather quickly have restored Christian political and religious dominance in France.

Only determinists will insist that second order counterfactuals will ultimately make alternative worlds converge with the real one. Karl Marx insisted that the triumph of liberal democracy and rising standards of living for the working class were inevitable consequences of capitalism. If Disraeli had not introduced social legislation in Britain, and if Henry Ford not pioneered profit sharing in America, other people would have done these things. Such claims are extreme, but they find an echo in biology where, ever since Darwin, it has been recognized that evolution produces morphological similitude because there is a best set of physical characteristics and strategy for grappling with the challenges of life. Diverse species have converged independently of the architectures and behavior most suited to avoiding predators and exploiting food resources (Morris, 1998).

I think it reasonable to assume that societies, like organisms, have a limited number of stable states. Accidents of history, real or counterfactual, can move the path of history away from these states, but there will be strong pressures to bring them back to the original or another stable state. Viewed in this light, the Mozart counterfactual is wanting in two respects. For reasons I have already made clear, it is the wrong counterfactual to produce the desired political consequent: a great power war in the early twentieth century. But even if some more appropriate counterfactual could produce that consequent, other developments -- second order counterfactuals -- would sooner or later have brought about the peaceful, developed, democratic and closely integrated Europe that we enjoy today.

Author's Reply

The reviewer completely misses the point. Of course, the Mozart counterfactual is far-fetched -- that's the whole idea! Erika is Germany's answer to Rube Goldberg. She or I could easily have provoked a European war by rewriting snippets of political history; Lebow and Tetlock did this, and convincingly for at least some of the historians they surveyed. Erika wanted to show how small, seemingly insignificant changes in reality can have large, unanticipated consequences across different domains. By doing this, she hoped to make readers aware of just how contingent, interconnected, and unpredictable the real world is. None of the more prosaic, and admittedly, more convincing, paths to war would have accomplished this goal.

The reviewer claims to refute the Mozart counterfactual on scientific grounds. I shared his arguments with Erika, and she dismissed them as *Quatsch* [poppycock]. After a long digression about the near-impossibility of multi-step counterfactuals, the reviewer concludes that what really matters is the probability of their individual steps, not their total number. The really telling question -- and here we agree with the reviewer -- is how to determine the probability of any step of any counterfactual. For some counterfactuals, this is pretty straight-forward. Epidemiologists have robust equations that describe the factors responsible for the spread of infectious diseases. They routinely conduct counterfactual experiments by altering the values of one or more terms of the equation to see how it would retard or facilitate the spread of particular pathogens. For political counterfactuals this is impossible; there are no general laws that we can apply to specific cases, or probabilities that we can calculate by observing the outcomes of a large number of similar events. Probability is a guessing game, and Erika's guesses are at least as good as the reviewer's.

When we strip away all the pseudo-science, the reviewer's prejudice is exposed. He or she is a crude determinist, no different from Karl Marx. The telling lines are the claims that culture could never influence economics or politics, but that economics determines politics. Does the reviewer offer any evidence for these assertions? None whatsoever. Many prominent historians believe that ideas determine the fundamental structure of any society's economics and politics, and that economics is a branch of political science devoted to analyzing how politics shape economic decisions. Surely, there is room for different points of views -- even in biology. At least one biologist, the American, Stephen Jay Gould, argued for the determining role of accident in evolution. He insisted that if you could rewind the tape of life and run the program over again you would end up with a radically different set of organisms each time (Gould, 1989).

The reviewer makes an admittedly good point about second order consequences. Changes in reality ripple through society in unpredictable ways -- this is a core assumption of the story. In theory, some other composer could have invented post-classicism. I acknowledge the need to add a paragraph or two to consider this problem in general, and to explain why Haydn was not close to becoming a post-classicist.

The Mozart counterfactual was meant to provoke and make readers think about the contingent nature of our world. If Erika had wanted to be more "scientific," she could have invited numerous counterfactuals that did not reach so far back into history and involved only minimal rewrites to provoke a European war. The same Lebow and Tetlock – the reviewer cites them *ad nauseum* – developed ten counterfactuals that could have led to a great power war in Europe in the first decades of the twentieth century. In their first counterfactual, the Congress of Vienna in 1815 awards Prussia land in Silesia and the Rhineland, where the industrial revolution got an early start and made possible Prussia's rise to great power status. Germany becomes unified under Prussian leadership, assumes an authoritarian character, and later in the nineteenth century pursues an aggressive foreign policy. The other counterfactuals are scattered throughout the nineteenth century, and several of them take place during or on the eve of the crisis that supposedly led to a European war. The more proximate the counterfactual to the war, the fewer the steps between antecedent and consequent. Lebow and Tetlock surveyed historians and they found some counterfactuals more plausible than others, and some of them likely to have produced the "desired" war. Most significantly, there was no correlation between their judgments and the number of steps these counterfactuals entailed.

I must warn you that Erika is very unhappy about this Luddite review. She is threatening to write a story in which soccer, not baseball, becomes the most popular European sport in the late nineteenth century. Just think of the political consequences! Police -- even those with helmets and leather jackets -- were loath to mess with protesting students and workers. A stone in the hands of a fastball pitcher can be lethal. Police vulnerability encouraged concession and compromise, which in turn helped facilitate democratic transitions in France and Germany. If soccer had become the rage, Europeans would have been good at kicking but terrible at throwing. You can't kick cobble stones at police from behind barricades. European police and political authorities would never have been intimidated by students and workers, and we might still be living under repressive, authoritarian regimes! Reviewers like this one might not have had the ability --- or the freedom -- to throw their metaphorical stones.